PRAISE FOR

*Songbird*

'I loved the story of Jamila and the resilience
and bravery of her family. Jamila is a wonderful
character, full of courage and heart, who children
will relate to and learn from.'
SALLY RIPPIN

'A beautiful story full of hope, heartache and love.'
ZANA FRAILLON

'Jamila is a wonderful character and I really loved
*Songbird*…It's a beautiful, hopeful story about digging
deep and helping those around you…a super-great read.'
FIONA HARDY

'A fun, tender and uplifting portrait of a young
Muslim girl's struggle to belong.'
*AEU MAGAZINE*

'An inspiring story…reading *Songbird* together is a
great way to start conversations with your children
about topical issues, refugees, and to help create
understanding around differences in culture and family.'
*BETTER READING*

'A gentle story about starting over, making friends
and finding a place in the world.'
*MAGPIES*

Ingrid Laguna lives in Melbourne. She teaches English to children from all over the world, many of whom have refugee backgrounds. *Songbird* is her first book for children.

# Ingrid Laguna

TEXT PUBLISHING MELBOURNE AUSTRALIA

textpublishing.com.au

The Text Publishing Company
Swann House, 22 William Street, Melbourne Victoria 3000, Australia

The Text Publishing Company (UK) Ltd
130 Wood Street, London EC2V 6DL, United Kingdom

Published by The Text Publishing Company, 2019.
Reprinted 2020.

Book design by Imogen Stubbs.
Cover illustration by GoodStudio / Shutterstock.
Typeset in Stempel Garamond 13/22pt by J&M Typesetting.

Printed and bound in Australia by Griffin Press, part of Ovato, an accredited ISO/NZS 14001:2004 Environmental Management System printer.

ISBN: 9781925773538 (paperback)
ISBN: 9781925774344 (ebook)

A catalogue record for this book is available from the National Library of Australia.

To the students of the
Collingwood English Language School,
for the privilege of sharing this part
of your journey. Your courage and
resilience have inspired this book.

# Chapter 1

Jamila paced the kitchen, feeding bread to her little brother, Amir, as she passed his highchair. Her hands kept moving—fiddling with the buttons on her school dress and re-pinning her headscarf. Jamila had been at her new school for three weeks, and she was trying hard to fit in. She missed her school in Iraq and her friends, especially Mina.

Today it was her turn to stand up at the front of her class and talk about herself. But it was hard to tell people in this new place about her old life. 'My name is Jamila,' she practised. 'I come...I

1

came to Australia because…' She didn't know how to explain it. There were things she could not say. She would just have to give the bare facts. 'We left our country, Iraq, because it was not safe for us there.'

'Just tell the class a few things about yourself,' Jamila's teacher, Miss Dana, had said. Miss Dana wore a stack of bracelets and scuffed red boots. Jamila liked her from day one. She let out big laughs and sat on the carpet with her students as if she was one of them. All the kids in Jamila's class gave a talk about themselves, not just Jamila, but Jamila felt different. What secrets could the other girls and boys have that were nearly as strange and shameful as hers?

'Mama—it's time to go!' called Jamila. She looked at her watch. Her father had given it to her the day she left Iraq.

'You will be safe in Australia,' he had said, crouching beside her, but Jamila saw the fear and worry in his eyes.

'You are brave, Jamila. Look after your mother. Help with Amir. I know you will. *Al Hamdu li'Allah.*' Praise God. Baba had slipped the watch off his wrist and put it on hers. It was too big and it hung loose. Jamila had to push it halfway up her arm and wedge it there.

It would be late afternoon in Baghdad now. Jamila wondered what Baba was doing. Was he on his way? He said he would come soon, but what did that mean—three days? Three weeks? Three months?

And what was Mina doing now? Jamila squeezed her eyes shut tight to send her thoughts to Mina. *Mina, are you okay?*

In her talk, Jamila wanted to tell the class about Mina, but how could she tell people she had only known for a few weeks that she had been wrenched away from her best friend in the world? And how would she explain that her father was not here and she didn't know when she would see him again? She could tell them he was coming soon. Jamila nodded to herself. She could say that. That felt good. She would say that in just a week, maybe two, he would be here.

But what would she say about her life with Mama and Amir? She didn't want anyone to know what that was like.

*My Mama goes to the market. She talks to people, makes friends. She brings home cake and strawberries. And she laughs. Always, she laughs.* That was what Jamila wanted to say, but it was mostly lies. She thought about her new song. Jamila liked to make up songs when she was scared or sad or worried, to take her away from the feelings.

Mama was lifting Amir from his highchair. '*Saeideeni!*' she called to Jamila. Help! Mama was fretting and she had that worried look. Jamila felt the familiar dread of what might lie ahead that day. She grabbed a cloth and wiped Amir's fingers.

'Come to Jamila,' she said. She picked him up and kissed his forehead. She tried to imagine standing in front of her class and telling them about looking after her baby brother. Today might be a good day for Mama to call Jamila home. Maybe then she would not have to give her class talk at all.

If I feel nervous, I'll breathe in through my nose for three seconds, then slowly out through my mouth, she reminded herself. (Her uncle Elias had taught her this when they were hiding in Baghdad.) If someone asks a question, I'll just answer, even if I have butterflies.

Jamila strapped Amir into his pram. 'It's time to go, Mama!' she called.

'I am coming.' Mama's voice sounded tired, as if it was just before bedtime, not morning. '*Habibty*,' Mama said, smiling weakly. My love.

Jamila put her bag over her shoulder and led

the way out the front door. There were kids' bikes lying flat in the concrete front yard of the house next door. A dog crossed the road nearby and Jamila hoped it had a home to go to. The air was cold, and she wriggled her fingers to keep them warm. She knew it was hot in Iraq. She remembered sitting under the shade of a wild oak with Mina and eating *bassbosa*, semolina cake, at the park in the hot, bright sun.

Maybe there were no soldiers in the street now and no shouting. Maybe Mina's mama and baba were not worrying and talking in whispers in the room next to Mina's. When Jamila had stayed at Mina's house for seven nights with Mama and Amir because Baba was away, she and Mina told each other stories. Jamila made some of those stories into songs and Mina called her *Mutraba*—a girl who is always singing—and sometimes she called her Songbird. Jamila missed Mina so much. She felt like a part of *her* was missing.

# Chapter 2

When Jamila arrived at school, the classroom heater whirred but she could not get warm. Winnie stood up the front for her talk. She said her mother was a vet nurse, and a girl behind Jamila said, 'Cool.' Winnie told the class that she had a cat called Fancy and that she had been doing tap classes since she was five. She didn't look nervous. She did a shoe-shuffling tap move and bowed to finish.

Now it was Jamila's turn. She went up to the front of the classroom. She looked at the faces peering up at her and wished she could see Mina there. Alice had one hand cupped to her mouth and she was whispering something. It made Jamila nervous. Was she saying something about her? Jamila's mama had called her home from school in the middle of the day twice already because she needed help at home. Jamila blushed when she thought about it. No one else in the class missed school to help at home.

Finn stared at Jamila with his chin in his palm and his yellow hair sticking out in all directions. Marco sat cross-legged beside Finn. His big brown eyes made Jamila's stomach flutter and she had to look away. Lan sat with her waiting face, and Georgia leant against a desk leg with her knees hugged to her chest. Beza, the only other girl in the class who wore a headscarf, stretched her legs out in front of her, scowling and picking at the carpet.

Jamila swallowed. In Baghdad, she was the best in her class at English, but now, in Australia, she fumbled her words. And she sometimes overheard other kids repeating what she had said and giggling.

'Good morning,' she said, taking a deep breath. 'My name is Jamila. I live in Reservoir with my mama...I mean my *mum*. And my brother.'

Finn re-crossed his legs and used his fingertips to prop his eyelids open as if he was so bored he would fall asleep.

Jamila felt uneasy. She put her hand on her dad's watch, and then she raised her voice.

'We came to Melbourne from Iraq two months ago. Iraq is a beautiful country. There are mountains, lakes, rivers. There is a golden mosque. And Baghdad...it is a big city. On hot nights, people eat ice-cream in the streets, and boys swim in the canal. There is a fun park with a big wheel covered in lights. There is music...drumming and singing. But also there are'—Jamila hesitated—'there are bombs.'

Finn sat up straight. Alice's eyes opened wide.

'They make a big noise,' said Jamila. 'And there are flashes of light.'

Lan's mouth fell open. Miss Dana looked worried, or sad, Jamila wasn't sure which.

'You hope they will be far off, or if they are close,' she said, 'you hope you can get away. People are scared. But...Iraq is a beautiful country.'

Jamila returned to her seat. She thought of all the wonderful things about Iraq. She remembered looking for treasures at the crowded markets, and the smell of spices. She could picture the giant sacks brimming with white beans and broad beans, and red and orange lentils. And the glittering river. Baba said Baghdad was once called the Jewel of the Islamic World.

Now it was Georgia's turn to stand up and speak. But Jamila hardly listened. She was worried. She had said too much. She wanted her classmates to understand her, and to like her. Jamila knew

Finn had chocolate spread on white bread in his lunch box most days and that Miranda was greeted at the end of each school day by her big brother and a dog called Leopold that only had three legs. She knew Lan preferred odd socks over matching ones and that Alice had glasses in her pencil case she slipped on at school pickup time. She knew who was friends with who and that she was still the new girl, after three whole weeks, who was not really friends with anyone.

Now, with her talk, had she made the space between her and everyone else even wider than it was before?

In silent reading that afternoon, Jamila chose a book about a girl whose mother was in the circus.

*Carmelina was an acrobat. She caught the rope as it swung towards her and sailed above the crowd. There were gasps and cheers and squeals of delight.*

'Ac-ro-bat,' whispered Jamila. She took out her dictionary booklet, flipped to the letter A and copied the word. Underneath, she wrote its meaning in her own language:

الشخص الذي يؤدي الحركات البهلوانية في السيرك

Jamila's Arabic words flowed onto the page. But writing in English was not easy. Jamila wondered if she would ever find English words easy. Lan's t's and l's were straight and neat. Her letters curled into one another and leant over together just right, with even spaces between the words. Speaking in English all day was hard too. Jamila had so much to say, but sometimes her mouth would open and close without a sound, like the fish caught by the boys on the Tigris River.

Lan was from China—how had she learnt to speak and write so well? Was there fighting in her country too? Maybe she and Lan could become friends. But Lan already knew a girl she ran to meet at recess and lunchtime and they shared their food and spoke their language together. If only Jamila knew one girl, or even a boy, who came from Iraq.

Georgia sat reading with her back to Jamila. The other kids at her table fidgeted. Georgia read at recess and lunchtime most days. Jamila wanted to talk to Georgia, but she didn't know what to say. Sometimes, at break times, Jamila walked briskly across the oval and zigzagged around the school buildings so that no one would notice that she was alone. She wondered whether Georgia read all the time for the same reason.

Yesterday, it was raining and Jamila had gone to the library and scoured the shelves as if she was trying to find a particular book. She heard kids in the Readers' Corner chatting and laughing and she wished she could be sitting with them, laughing too. She only felt worse when the librarian offered to help her find the book she wasn't even really looking for.

Picking up her dictionary booklet, Jamila bit down on her lip and approached Georgia. 'Hi,' she said. She pointed in her dictionary booklet to where she had written *acrobat*. 'How do you say this?'

Georgia pushed her glasses up the bridge of her nose. 'Acrobat,' she said, and she turned back to her book.

'Acrobat,' said Jamila.

'*Mm-hm.*'

'Oh...thanks,' Jamila said. She stayed beside Georgia, squeezing her toes in her shoes. 'What are you reading?' she asked at last.

Georgia flipped over the cover of her book. She didn't look up.

Jamila read: '*The Day the Sun Ref...Ref...*'

'Refused to Shine,' said Georgia. '*The Day the Sun Refused to Shine.*'

'That looks hard. I mean...good...but hard to read. Is it? Is it hard?'

Georgia shook her head. 'No.'

'I'm reading...' Jamila began, but she couldn't remember the name of her book. She felt her cheeks go hot. Just then, Miss Dana clapped twice and told everyone to sit down. She had been cranky that morning, surprising everyone by smacking her hand down onto her desk when Winnie couldn't stop laughing. At least she didn't smack students. Not ever. Not like some teachers in Baghdad. Jamila's shoe made an embarrassing squeak against the floor as she swivelled away from Georgia to go back to her desk.

Silent reading was over. Jamila took out her copy of *Further than the Moon*, the book the whole class was reading.

'We were talking about *where* the story happens,' announced Winnie.

Jamila saw Finn look at Marco and let his jaw drop and his eyes roll back. Her heart still thumped from trying to talk to Georgia. She gripped her pen and kept her eyes down.

'Yes, Winnie,' said Miss Dana. 'But please, don't call out.'

'The girl...Maddi, she lives in Darwin,' said Alice.

Miss Dana looked tired. She pressed her fingertips to her forehead. 'You're right, Alice.' She looked like she didn't care if the story was set in Darwin or the Zagros Mountains. She reminded Jamila of Mama. Jamila knew her mama spent the nights worrying for Baba. The same worry kept Jamila awake at night too. Baba had spent time in jail for writing news stories about what was happening in Iraq. He was not locked up anymore, but he was still writing stories, so he had to hide all the time. How much longer would they have to wait for him to come?

It was night time in Iraq now. The world was spinning slowly: Jamila had the sun, so Baba had the moon. As long as Jamila was in Australia and

Baba was in Iraq, they would never both have the sun or the moon at the same time.

Miss Dana's voice was tight and it cut across the room. 'I really need you to put up your hand if you have something to say, okay?' It sounded like a question you weren't supposed to answer. No one did. Jamila had never called out. She couldn't remember the last time she had a mouth full of words that couldn't wait to come out.

Jamila wondered what kind of problems Miss Dana might have. She was in her own country where just about everyone spoke her language. She had probably never spent time in a bomb shelter trying not to inhale the smell of sweat and fear of the strangers squishing against her.

Miss Dana asked why Maddi, in the story, had run away from home.

Jamila had read the whole book. And she had written new words and their meanings in her dictionary booklet. There were oil and tomato stains on some pages where she had been writing while she ate. But she couldn't think of the right words to answer the question.

Georgia's hand went up. In Iraq, it used to be Jamila's hand going up. She always knew the answers. She was a good student. Baba used to listen to her read after school.

'Baba.' Jamila mouthed the word soundlessly, her eyes hot with tears.

Georgia's words poured out smoothly like cream into a bowl. Then it was Alice's turn. Her sentences were good too. Jamila felt mute, like her mouth was useless. Her chair scraped the floor as she turned to face the window, to look outside where there was no Georgia, no Alice and no questions she couldn't find the words to answer. She remembered Miss Eeda, her teacher in Iraq, holding up her work to show the rest of the class. She remembered feeling confident when she handed in homework. She did not feel good, this new Jamila.

# Chapter 3

Jamila kept looking at the classroom clock, willing the morning recess bell to ring. She could not think of a word to describe herself that started with the first letter of her name. *Just. Joke. Jealous.* Georgia and Winnie were already pinning their name poems on the display board when Miss Dana appeared beside her. Was she going to tell her that Mama had called? Jamila felt panic creep over her. It wasn't even lunchtime yet. *Not again, Mama, no.*

Jamila quickly moved her hand to cover the

empty space beside the letters of her name. She hadn't wanted to use the dictionary because nobody else had. But Miss Dana moved Jamila's hand aside. '*Hmm*, J is a hard one,' she said.

Jamila guessed it wasn't *actually* hard. She wished Miss Dana wouldn't do that. She wasn't five years old. English just wasn't her real language.

'Let's see. Gentle?' said Miss Dana. 'No, that starts with G. Jovial? That means happy.' Jamila didn't see herself as happy. She used to. She remembered Baba's face lighting up when she skipped into the kitchen in the mornings. She was always happy when they played cards on Sunday mornings and when she took a basket of *klecha* biscuits she'd made herself to Mina's house.

'What do you think?' asked Miss Dana. 'Jovial?'

'Okay,' said Jamila.

'Jovial Jamila. Very good.' Then Miss Dana told Jamila that her mother had called the school.

*Wallah!* Jamila knew it.

'You need to go home,' said Miss Dana. 'For an appointment.'

Jamila had written some English words on bits of paper and stuck them above the kettle and on the bathroom mirror to help Mama learn. She imagined her trying out the words before making the call. 'Home.' 'Now.' 'Appointment.' Mama had not mentioned any appointments that morning to Jamila.

Jamila looked away from Miss Dana to hide her face. Then she stood up and packed up her things.

Jamila waited in the school foyer. Mama would come with Amir by bus to collect her. Winnie and Alice walked past with their arms linked. Winnie glanced at Jamila, then whispered something to Alice, who murmured back. Were they talking about Jamila? Jamila was sure they were.

Three weeks ago, on Jamila's first day, Alice

was chosen to show Jamila around the school, and together they walked along the corridors while Alice pointed out the toilets, the library, the art room and the sick bay. Alice's face was bright and her voice was warm. Jamila hoped she and Alice would become friends. But when the tour was finished, Alice returned to the friends she already had and that was the end of that.

In the cold air of the foyer, Jamila pulled her cardigan tight around her. She thought of Sara, a girl at her school in Iraq, who took deep, sucking breaths from a rattling asthma pump and pinched at the skin on her wrists. The other kids left her alone. Jamila once saw her leaning against the school gate half-hidden by a tree. She was just standing there, breaking twigs from its branches. Now Jamila knew how Sara felt—like Jamila did now. Like everyone else *had* someone. Everyone except her.

She wondered what Mama needed her for

this time. Had Amir hurt himself and Mama did not have enough English to make a doctor's appointment? Had letters been delivered that she could not read? Did she need Jamila to go to the ATM to take money out for her? Perhaps there was news of Baba.

In Baghdad, Mama had once picked up a giant bird with a broken wing and carried it from the road to the grass. Mama volunteered at the bird sanctuary. There was an eagle called Fadhil that perched on Mama's outstretched arm while it pecked at bread from her free hand. Jamila felt like that Mama was a different person.

Mama finally arrived. She looked nervously around as she stood at the school entrance.

'Here!' called Jamila. She ran to Mama, hung her bag over the pram and took over pushing it as they left the school. That afternoon, Jamila would miss maths and drama. At least she was good at maths. She didn't need perfect English for that. But she did need to practise her part in the play they were rehearsing in drama. She hated the stumbling way she read her lines. Finn groaned each time it was her turn to read, which made Jamila lose her spot altogether.

Sitting on the bus beside Mama, Jamila put in her headphones and listened to her favourite singer, Kathem Al Saher. 'Acrobat,' she whispered to herself, fogging the window.

She missed her old life. She wished she could see Mina and tell her everything. She closed her eyes and pretended she was on a ferry crossing the Tigris River. She saw the palm trees along its banks, and imagined she was with Mina on her way to Al-Nahar Street where there were donkey carts and the shop windows glittered with gold.

'We need to buy food,' said Mama.

'Oh...okay,' Jamila said. She wished Mama didn't need her for such a simple thing. She noticed new creases fanning out from the corners of Mama's eyes, as if she was a person who laughed a lot. But she hardly ever laughed now.

'And English class,' said Mama, interrupting Jamila's thoughts. 'Today—shopping and I have English class.'

'Really?' asked Jamila. She didn't know her mama was going to English classes.

Mama sighed. 'I try,' she said. She pinched her mouth shut. She looked scared. Jamila thought of Carmelina, the acrobat in the book, sailing fearlessly over the circus crowd and wished Mama was like she used to be. And Baba. Where was he? Staying with Uncle Elias in Karbala? Or hiding in the mountains? Did he have food and a bed to sleep in?

Back home, Jamila sang to herself to stop the worry humming in her chest. She remembered Mina calling her *Songbird*, and her heart clenched with missing her friend. She changed her clothes and Amir's nappy and dropped the house keys into her bag.

'*Yalla*, Mama. Let's go.' They had not been home long, but it was better to keep moving.

Jamila helped Mama to unpack the shopping when they returned. Then she went to her room and wrote in her notebook.

*Thursday 20 August 2015*
*I wish we could shop at the bazaar like we used to. Maybe then Mama would smile again. This is not our home. I miss walking the alleys of clucking chickens with Mama and Baba, and Amir on Baba's shoulders. I want to smell the spices and see the watermelons stacked in a pyramid and fish laid out in rows. I want to hear my language everywhere, like music all around me.*

*Everything is different now. Mama used to push me to keep up with my schoolwork and to read books at night. Now, I take myself to my room to do my homework. I have more freedom than before and sometimes that's a good thing. I can go to and from school by myself and stop at the park or the shop on the way. But I don't know Reservoir like I know Kadhimiya in Baghdad. One time I got lost and it took ages to find our street. I was scared. I miss my home. I miss my country.*

Jamila went with Mama to her English class that afternoon. They sat on green plastic chairs in a corridor while they waited. Other people were waiting too. They spoke to one another in languages Jamila didn't understand. A woman came over. She smiled shyly at Mama. She said her name was Zainab and that she came from Iraq. Mama and Zainab spoke in Arabic, taking each other's hands and holding on. They swapped phone numbers and hugged. Mama had a friend of her own now. That was something.

# Chapter 4

The corridor to Jamila's classroom was filled with kids chattering and jostling when she arrived at school the next morning. Jamila couldn't see anyone she could talk to. She spotted a flyer pinned to the wall and was grateful for an excuse to stand alone while she read:

*Grade 5/6 Choir Starts This Week*
*After school every Wednesday*
*In the Multipurpose Hall*
*Questions: See Ms Carrington*

Jamila held her breath as she read it again. She loved to sing more than anything. No one had told her there might be a choir at her school. Her body hummed the way it did when she ran fast, even though she was standing still. She wished she could tell Mina about the school choir. She wished she could tell anyone.

'Singing is *haram*. No good for Muslim girl.' The words were thrown hotly at Jamila. Beza had appeared suddenly. She stood tall as if she had more answers than questions. From her class talk, Jamila knew that Beza came from Ethiopia and that she was also Muslim. But who was Beza to tell Jamila what she could and could not do?

Mama and Baba told stories of Jamila singing from the age of two—in the bath, in the kitchen while Mama prepared *samoon* bread, and on the long drive from Baghdad to Karbala. When Jamila and her family had to hide in a bomb shelter, Jamila sang softly, and the frightened gathering went quiet.

When they came out into the daylight, a woman with a baby bundled against her chest took Jamila's hand. '*Shukraan*,' she said. Thank you.

Jamila locked eyes with Beza. 'Singing is good. My baba says it is not *haram* if it makes people feel—'

Beza brought her face close to Jamila's. She smelled of cloves and chewing gum. 'Your baba is not here,' she said.

'He is coming,' said Jamila.

'*Hmph.*'

Jamila wanted to kick Beza's shin, to send her fist flying into her jaw. Instead, she thought about the choir as she strode away. *Wednesday after school. Two sleeps.* She knew what Mina would say: 'You are *Mutraba*. You are Songbird.'

But Beza had scared her, and Jamila's heart drummed in her chest.

When Jamila joined the choir that Wednesday,

she sang out—clean and clear. The more she sang, the better she felt. Difference didn't matter—what you wore or where your father was or how you pronounced your words. Ms Carrington told everyone where to stand, no matter who was friends with who. No matter who was popular and who was not.

Beams crisscrossed the hall ceiling and a high window ran the length of the back wall. There was an old piano, a whiteboard on wheels, and the smell of paint coming from the art room next door.

Jamila counted eight students at the first choir session, then ten at the second, and by the third week there were twelve in the group. Wednesday became Jamila's favourite day, and when she was not at choir, she was singing the songs softly to herself or to Amir and Mama at home.

In the third week of choir, Ms Carrington made

an announcement. 'There will be auditions for the solo parts for the end-of-term concert.'

'What is *solo*?' Jamila blurted.

Finn coughed up a nasty laugh but Jamila only blinked.

'Solo means by oneself,' said Ms Carrington. Her skirt matched her blazer and her blazer matched her shoes. 'It means, one person sings, accompanied only by the piano.'

'On stage?' asked Jamila. 'In front of the audience?' Fizziness spread inside her.

'In front of the audience,' said Ms Carrington. 'Auditions will be held in the music room at lunchtime next Tuesday.'

Jamila's mind began to race as she made her way from the hall. She wanted to perform a solo. She would fill the space with her voice, she would sing past the ceiling and through the windows into the schoolyard. Mama would remember Jamila had a gift. Georgia and Alice and Winnie and Finn would see what she could do. Miss Dana would gasp with surprise. This was her chance.

On the morning of the audition day, Jamila could not concentrate. Her hands twisted in her lap. What if Mama called her home from school? She wouldn't go. She would refuse. She wondered what she would have to do in the audition. Who else was going for the solo parts?

Jamila's gaze flicked from the numbers on the page to her watch and the wall clock and back. She heard the words 'audition' and 'solo' in snippets of chatter around her, and her palms felt damp. When Miss Dana asked her to put seven-tenths into a decimal, she stared blankly.

Outside at recess, an aeroplane appeared in the distance. Jamila imagined she was on that plane and flying to Baghdad. She saw herself running down the path to the front door of her house and Baba standing in the doorway, waiting just for her.

She wanted to tell him about the audition.

'*In shaa Allah*, it will be you,' he would say.

When the lunch bell finally rang, Jamila had already packed up her folder and books. She arrived at the music room at the same time as another student, a new girl in the other grade five class. She had a birthmark across one cheek, and her school dress seemed to float over her delicate body. She held a wooden flower press under one arm and the air around her was quiet and still. She reminded Jamila of Mina.

'Are you here to audition?' asked Jamila. 'For a solo?'

The girl nodded and shuffled her shoe. 'I love singing,' she said.

'I love singing too!' The words escaped Jamila's mouth in a rush. 'More than anything.'

The girl smiled shyly. 'My name is Eva.'

Jamila pressed her hand to her chest. 'I'm Jamila. You're new here—you should join the choir.'

'We've just moved, from Sydney.'

'I have been here...maybe...' Jamila counted the weeks on her fingers. 'Nearly three months now.' She remembered the goodbyes: the scratchy wool of Baba's jumper as he hugged her tight, Mina's tear-streaked face in the crowded airport, and watching the ground grow distant as the plane flew her away from everything and everyone she knew.

'I only found out we were coming to Australia one week before we left,' said Jamila.

Eva's eyes grew large. 'One week? How did you have time to get ready?'

'We were waiting for visas...to get away. Waiting and waiting. Then one day, the phone rang, and they said we could come. We just packed some clothes...just a few things. We were happy, Mama and me, and sad too. We would be safe from the fighting and the danger. But we had to leave Baba—my dad.'

'Leave your dad. Why?' asked Eva.

Jamila looked out the window to think. 'He will come soon,' she said.

There was the click and fuzz of the loudspeaker coming on and a request for someone to go to the front office. It was not Mama calling Jamila home, but every time the loudspeaker clicked on, she tensed up, just in case.

'So now you are here,' said Eva.

'And now *you* are here too,' said Jamila. 'Maybe we can sing a solo together!'

'Which makes it a duet,' said Eva. 'Even better.' She held up her palm and Jamila high-fived it. Eva brought her hands together and looked to the ceiling. 'Please, please, please,' she said. 'I promise I'll tidy my room and do my homework and set the table.'

Jamila pressed her palms together too. 'And I will help Mama and look after Amir and do my Salat prayers every day,' she said. *'Bismillahir Rahmanir Raheem.'*

'Huh?'

'In the name of Allah,' said Jamila. She laughed and realised that had become a rare sound. 'I come from Iraq. It's my language, Arabic.'

'I've heard of Iraq,' said Eva. 'But I've never been there. I've been to Tasmania and New Zealand.'

Jamila wondered what Eva had heard about Iraq. She thought about telling her about the music and dancing and delicious food, but sometimes it was easier not to talk about her country at all. Jamila asked Eva why she had come to Melbourne.

'My dad got a job here,' said Eva. 'He's a pilot.'

'My dad's a journalist,' said Jamila. 'He writes news reports.' Jamila thought she might be a journalist one day. A singer and a journalist. 'Sometimes,' she said, 'Baba has been in trouble because of his work. When he wrote about the fighting.'

Jamila tried not to think about the time Baba was taken away by angry men. The sight and smell of his dark and scary prison cell hovered in her mind.

'Is that why he is not here?' asked Eva. Jamila felt a spike of worry. She didn't want to talk about it. She looked away.

'Jamila from Iraq,' said Eva gently.

'Eva from Sydney,' said Jamila, and a smile passed between them.

Side by side, Jamila and Eva approached the music room door and peered in. The heater was whirring in a corner and Jamila could smell lavender. Ms Carrington sat at the piano.

'We are here for the audition,' said Jamila. She had chosen and practised two songs she had written herself, one in Arabic, the other in English. One was bright, the other slow and sorrowful. They were songs that showed the way she could sing from high notes to low ones.

'Good,' said Ms Carrington. 'Enthusiasm and punctuality.' She placed her hands into her lap, carefully, as if they were precious, and turned to Jamila. 'Come and stand here where I can hear you.' Jamila worried that Ms Carrington might hear the thuds of her heart.

'We won't be long,' said Ms Carrington to Eva. 'Please wait outside, and close the door.'

Eva pulled the door until it clicked shut.

'Now, Jamila, I will play a note...' Her expression was serious. 'You sing it back and hold it. All right?'

Ms Carrington played a note and Jamila took a breath, closed her eyes and sang. 'La...' There was a stretch of silence before Ms Carrington played another note and Jamila sang it back.

'Okay,' said Ms Carrington.

Jamila tried to read her tone—did she detect disappointment? She couldn't be sure.

Ms Carrington played a key towards the

bottom end of the keyboard. Jamila dropped her chin to her chest to sing the low note.

'All done,' said Ms Carrington.

All done? All *done*?!

'But, I want to sing,' said Jamila. Her songs were waiting on the tip of her tongue.

'No need, Jamila. Grade and teacher?' Ms Carrington jotted down some notes.

'Grade five. My teacher is Miss Dana. I…'

'Thank you.'


There was a fidgety line of students waiting outside the door. Eva was at the front, brushing the end of her ponytail over her lips. 'How was it?' she asked.

'Short,' said Jamila, crossly. 'I didn't get time to sing my songs. Not one!'

'Next, please!' called Ms Carrington. Eva's eyebrows pushed together.

'It's okay—go!' said Jamila.

Eva drew herself up and disappeared through the door.

Jamila felt a tug on her sleeve. It was Georgia.

'What did you have to do?' asked Georgia, her gaze slipping away from Jamila's.

*Khajula*, thought Jamila. Shy. It was usually Jamila asking Georgia questions. She wanted to give her a good answer.

'You don't have to do much,' she said. 'You just sing some notes.'

'Oh?' said Georgia, looking worried. 'I probably shouldn't be here.' Pink splotches appeared on her neck. 'I don't think I'm a good singer.' Georgia always sang softly in choir. She wasn't confident singing.

'Well,' said Jamila. 'Ms Carrington plays a note on the piano, and you listen …and…'

Winnie and Alice joined them. Jamila saw Georgia hold her book closer against her chest.

'You listen and then sing the note,' said Jamila.

'That's all.'

Georgia's brows made a V-shape. 'No scales?' she asked.

'No, no scales,' said Jamila.

'No hymns?' asked Winnie. Jamila had never heard the word. She shook her head.

She wanted to go back into the music room. She wanted to sing her songs.

'Or the national anthem?' asked Alice. 'Or, I don't know, "Over the Rainbow"?'

'No. Just notes.' Jamila kicked the floor and shook her head. 'No songs.'

# Chapter 5

Jamila and Eva sat together to eat lunch after the auditions, though Jamila was still mad and not very hungry. How could Ms Carrington know how well she could sing from just three notes? They made their way to the playground over grass that was slick with mud. Their shoes squelched. Jamila looked around for Marco but couldn't see him anywhere. She was glad at first, and then disappointed.

Finn kicked a soccer ball nearby. 'Hey Jamila,' he called out. 'How come you're always wearing that thing on your head?'

'I'm not *always*,' she said. 'I take it off when I'm at home.'

'Why not at school?' asked Finn.

Jamila rolled her eyes. What business was it of his? 'Because I'm not allowed,' she said.

'Why not?' asked Finn.

She turned her whole body to face him. 'In my country,' she said, 'Lots of Muslim girls don't show their hair to boys or men if they're not family.'

'That's weird,' said Finn. 'Why not?'

Finn said 'weird' a lot: to describe food in other people's lunch boxes or to describe people when he didn't know what else to call them.

'It's not weird,' said Jamila. '*You're* weird.'

'I'm not the one wearing a scarf on my head the whole entire time.'

Jamila folded her arms. 'It's called a *hijab*. And I *like* to wear it. And where I come from, many Muslim girls wear hijabs.'

'What's Muslim?' asked Finn.

'It's…'

'Whatever,' said Finn. 'Have you even got hair?'

Eva elbowed Jamila. 'Swings?' she said.

'I'll race you!' said Jamila, breaking into a run up the hill.

Jamila and Eva propelled themselves into the air on the swings. The higher they went, the more it felt like flying. Jamila sang into the wind. Maybe her days of hiding and eating lunch by herself were in the past. Maybe she could tell Eva about her life outside school, about Mama needing her help all the time. Their swings crossed paths mid-air. Jamila imagined grabbing Eva's hands and doing a circus trick. In the distance, she saw Georgia heading into the library.

'Do you think Georgia reads a lot to hide her shyness?' said Jamila, flinging her legs out in front of her.

'Maybe,' said Eva. 'Hey, look!'

Miss Dana was striding towards them.

*Please, no, Mama*, Jamila thought. *Please, not today.*

Miss Dana waved as she approached and Jamila waved back. She scuffed the ground with her shoe and brought the swing to a stop. Miss Dana's hair was tied up high in a messy knot. She wore pinstriped pants and she had a green ring on her thumb.

Jamila kept her face smooth.

'Your mother rang,' said Miss Dana. 'She needs you at home.'

Jamila's anger rose up in her like a fever. It wasn't only Mama who was trying to live in a new country. Jamila was too. This was absolutely not helping.

'Oh,' said Jamila, trying to hide her feelings as she slipped off the swing. 'Okay.' She said it lightly, as if she didn't mind Mama calling her home.

All her life, Jamila had been taught that family was number one. *Look after your mother*, Baba had said. *Help with Amir.* But what about Jamila's new friendship with Eva? Wasn't that important too? And what about her science project? If only there were two of her: one Jamila at home to help Mama, and the other at school with her new friend.

Jamila collected her schoolbag and waited in the foyer. Mama finally arrived and they made their way to the bus stop. When the bus came, Jamila helped Mama to lift the pram up the steps.

'Why do I have to come home?' asked Jamila. 'Why?'

Jamila knew Winnie missed school when her cat was hit by a car. Georgia had missed school to go to the eye doctor two Mondays in a row. But Jamila was the only one missing school to help her mother.

The bus rumbled along the now-familiar streets, past the shop that smelt like sour milk, where Jamila bought caramello koalas sometimes. And past the falling-down house on the corner that Jamila wanted to explore one day.

'A man rang this morning,' said Mama.

'What man?' said Jamila.

'I couldn't understand him. If he calls again, you can talk to him and tell me what he says.'

Jamila sat up straight. 'Did he ring about Baba? What did he say?'

'He said Baba's name,' said Mama. 'But I don't know who he was or what he wanted. He said my name and Baba's name and he asked me questions and—'

'Maybe he is asking for our address, so he can tell Baba where to find us!'

Two seats in front of them, a man held a baby girl at his shoulder. He hummed a tune and patted her back. Jamila watched her rest her chin on his shoulder and her eyes slow-blink until they closed.

'Did you ask for his phone number?' Jamila asked.

'No.'

'Mama!'

'He will call again. Then we will know.'

They passed the apartment block with the big iron gates that reminded Jamila of the museum Baba used to take her to in Baghdad. She hoped the phone would ring as soon as she walked in the door.

But when they arrived home, the apartment was cold and sunless and the phone was as silent as midnight. Amir began to cry. Jamila wiped his tears with her thumb. She kissed him and cooed until his cries turned to hiccups, all the while hoping for the phone to ring. She wondered if any of the girls at school looked after their little brothers or sisters as much as she did. She felt a tightening in her chest and so she sang softly, close to Amir's ear.

Mama was writing a shopping list. She wrote: بيلح.

Jamila took the pen from her hand and wrote the same word in English: milk. 'Milk,' she said. She wanted to help Mama learn.

'*Lays al'an,*' said Mama, with a flick of her wrist. Not now.

Jamila went to her room. If Mama didn't improve her English, she would always need Jamila's help. The words of a song Jamila had begun to write looped in her head and she sang to herself:

*There is an old pistachio tree in my garden far away*
*Climb into its branches, say hello from me*

That afternoon, as Jamila helped Mama hang out the washing, she told her about school, about choir and about Eva, pushing words out into the silence. She wanted Mama to think about something other than Baba. When the washing was done, Jamila swept the floor. Then she prepared *shabbat*

51

chicken. She kept looking at the phone. She hoped for any kind of news of Baba, or a way to help him to come.

When dinner was ready, Mama only picked at her food, and she looked to the door as if expecting someone. Jamila huffed air through her nose and went to her room.

Why hadn't Mama asked for the man's phone number? What was wrong with her?

Jamila wished she could talk to Mina.

That night, Jamila heard Mama on the phone to her one friend, Zainab. She said that a man had called from Immigration asking about Kasim. Jamila's heart skidded hearing Baba's name. She pressed her ear to the wall, listening hard. Mama told Zainab she didn't know if Baba was on his way or if he had been captured. A sob caught in Mama's throat. '*La naerif 'ayu shay*,' she said. We don't know anything.

# Chapter 6

Even though her clock said it was 7:49am, and a square of morning sunlight lay on her doona, Jamila was not ready to get up. She had been anxious through the night, trying to keep bad thoughts away. She dragged herself out of bed and got dressed for school. She could not hear Mama moving around the house.

She fed and dressed Amir. Still no Mama.

She went into Mama's room and opened blinds and windows. Mama lay sleeping. Her hair covered her face, as if she was trying to hide.

'Do you want coffee?' said Jamila.

Mama's eyes flipped open as if Jamila's voice had frightened her awake. She held a hand up to shield her eyes from the light. 'Jamila?'

'I have to go to *school*,' said Jamila. 'Do you want me to get you coffee? To help you wake up?'

'No, Jamila.' Mama sat up. 'I'm awake now.' She touched a finger to Jamila's nose. 'Go,' she said.

*Please don't call me home from school today*, thought Jamila, though she didn't say it. She pinched Amir's cheeks. '*Habibi*,' she said. My love. She kissed him three times and bolted out the door.

Jamila was tired on the bus ride to school, her eyelids fought to stay open. She had not slept well. She kept thinking about the man on the phone. Had they missed a chance to help Baba come?

When the bus arrived at school, Jamila

54

checked her watch: 8:57. *'Ya Rab!'* Oh, God. She jumped out and ran through the gates and into her building. As she turned into the corridor to her classroom, she almost crashed into a huddle of girls and boys. They were peering at a sheet of paper on the noticeboard.

'Jamila!' Eva shouted, splitting from the group and coming towards her. 'Our names are there! We got the solo parts!'

Jamila felt sparks go through her.

'Come and see,' said Eva. She and Jamila weaved through the other kids. 'There!'

Jamila saw her name, as well as Eva's. She wanted to shoot her fists into the air and shout praise to Allah, but she kept it all inside. *'Mudahash,'* she whispered. Amazing.

Jamila thought of Mina. Whenever Jamila had good news or bad, questions or problems, she always told Mina. When Baba was taken away by prison guards, Jamila had called Mina. And when she found out he was finally being released, it was Mina who shared her happiness and hugged her tight.

Jamila tried to picture Mina's face, and to remember the sound of her voice.

Jamila wanted to tell Baba her news too. He might have danced in the kitchen, lifted her into the air. She imagined his smile so big it pulled at the corners of his eyes, just like it was when she sang for the whole family when they celebrated Eide and the end of Ramadan.

When Jamila arrived home from school that day, she found Mama in the courtyard.

'I'm singing a solo!' she called out, slamming the front door behind her. She ran to Mama. '*Binafsi*, Mama!' By myself!

Mama tilted her head to one side and brushed Jamila's cheek. '*Abnatay aldhakiya*,' she said. My clever girl. Her words were soft and her smile was thin. The look in her eyes was far away.

'It's a solo, Mama!' said Jamila. 'Only Eva and I are singing solos!'

'*Ah'santi*, Jamila.' Well done.

Jamila could tell it was not one of Mama's good days.

'And also, I think Eva is my best friend now, Mama. I mean—second best, after Mina. And I think I will sing her my new song tomorrow, the one about our pistachio tree.'

'*Hmm*,' said Mama. Jamila could tell Mama wasn't really listening.

Jamila turned away and scooped up Amir. 'A solo, *habibi*,' she told him softly. 'I'm singing a solo.'

That evening, while Jamila kneaded dough to make flatbread and while she swished her bath water into a tower of bubbles, she thought about Mina. The distance between her and Mina was like a giant creature whose arms went for miles, who refused to listen to small girls with big news. Or mothers without their husbands. Or fathers too far from their daughters to hear them sing.

At bedtime, Jamila sat cross-legged in her pyjamas and jotted down words. She turned them into phrases. Before long, she had a page of them. She hummed a melody and made up a chorus that rose and dipped. She stayed up until she could no longer fight off sleep. And then she dreamed that she told Mina her news, and her friend beamed with happiness as if *she* was singing the solo.

Jamila woke up feeling peaceful. Her song lyrics were in the notebook beside her bed. All her tangled feelings were now written on the page. The song's title was at the top: 'My Faraway'.

# Chapter 7

Jamila was drinking from the water fountain when Alice and Winnie came over.

'Hey,' said Alice. 'We saw you got a solo part.'

'Yes,' said Jamila. 'I still can't believe it.'

'Sing something,' said Winnie. There was spite in Winnie's voice.

'Sing what?' said Jamila. Why was Winnie asking her to sing right now, in the schoolyard?

'We just want to hear you sing,' said Winnie.

Winnie had heard Jamila singing in the choir every week. What did she really want?

'No,' said Jamila. 'I don't want to.' She wished the bell would ring so they would have to go to class.

'We're not saying you're *not* a good singer,' said Alice. 'But maybe you got the part because you're, you know, the new girl. From another country.'

'What do you mean?' said Jamila, looking from one girl to the other. 'That's not true.'

'Ms Carrington just feels sorry for you,' said Winnie.

'She does not.' A small storm built in the pit of Jamila's stomach.

'Yes,' said Alice. 'She does.'

'I know I can sing well,' said Jamila. 'I am Songbird.'

'So sing something, Songbird,' said Winnie.

Jamila stuck the toe of her shoe into the wet sand at the base of the fountain and flicked it into the air. It only just missed Winnie's shoe as it landed. She did it again and a dollop of sand hit

Alice's dress before plopping to the ground. Alice shrieked and stepped back.

Now Jamila wished Mama *would* call her home. Immediately. She turned around and ran in the direction of the library. She wanted to hide away.

Jamila managed to avoid Winnie and Alice for the rest of the morning. At recess, she told Eva what had happened and together they decided they needed a secret getaway spot. They gathered pebbles from along the fence to make a circle of their own in a hidden corner of the schoolyard—a place they would always know where to find each other. When Beza came over and asked what they were doing, Jamila shrugged. 'Nothing interesting,' she said, slipping pebbles into her pockets. The three girls stood awkwardly, saying nothing, until Beza turned and walked away.

At lunchtime, Jamila saw Beza talking to Miss

Melanie, the teacher on yard duty, and pointing to her and Eva.

'What is she saying?' said Eva.

'I don't know,' said Jamila, trying to read Beza's lips. 'But I do know she doesn't think Muslim girls should sing in the choir.'

Miss Melanie called Jamila and Eva over. She was usually friendly. But today her words were sharp. 'Beza tells me you are refusing to include her,' she said.

'No,' Jamila began. 'We were just—'

'We didn't—' said Eva.

A tear slipped from the corner of Beza's eye and she did nothing to wipe it away.

'Beza is clearly upset,' said Miss Melanie. 'Is there something you would like to say to her?'

'Sorry?' ventured Jamila, her voice rising with the question. She did not believe Beza's tears were real.

'You're not asking her a question,' said Miss

Melanie. 'You need to be properly sorry. You must not exclude people.'

Adults always thought things were black and white, right and wrong. Jamila knew it was not that simple. It was Beza who was unkind. It was Beza who should be sorry.

'I'm sorry,' said Jamila. She was sorry that Beza did not know how to make friends.

'Okay,' said Beza softly, looking down at her shoes.

'Thank you, Jamila,' said Miss Melanie, and then she sighed as she turned and walked away.

Jamila and Eva watched her go. Jamila wondered if Miss Melanie had a husband or any children. Jamila's teacher in Baghdad stopped coming to school for a long time when her son was killed. He had been walking home from school when a bomb inside a car exploded near him. When Miss Eeda returned the following term, she looked different, even though she was wearing the same hijab with the diamonds on it, and the same blue cardigan. She looked like she wasn't sure which way was home, as if she was walking in circles in a room with no light.

'Miss Melanie thinks we're mean,' said Eva, holding her palms out in front of her as a fine mist of rain started to fall. 'And now it's raining and my hair will go curly. It's not fair.'

'Nothing is fair,' said Jamila, kicking up dirt with her shoe. It was not fair that Jamila was safe in Australia while Mina was most definitely not safe in Iraq. And it was not fair that Baba's life was in danger because he wrote about things that were true. Jamila tilted her head back and stuck out her tongue just like she used to do with Mina when it rained. There was a sudden clap of thunder and then the rain came down hard and fast. Jamila and Eva ran for shelter.

# Chapter 8

At the next choir session, Ms Carrington sat facing a semicircle of empty chairs. The hall window framed a blue winter sky.

Jamila was excited. She would be singing a solo. She patted the seat beside her when she saw Eva arrive. Alice and Winnie moved to the centre seats, and Finn stood in the doorway, shifting from foot to foot like he was plugged into the wall and switched on. When Marco arrived, the two boys took turns grinding their knuckles into each other's shoulders.

Jamila tried to think of just-right things to say to Marco. Whenever they were in the same group for classwork, Jamila's mind ran in circles. *What are you reading?* No, that was no good—he only read a book if he had to, because it was school. *Have you finished the solar system project?* Boring. *Do you like playing soccer?* Dumb question. He obviously loved soccer. What did she *want* to say to him? *I am Jamila. I'm over here!*

Ms Carrington stood up. 'Thank you to everyone who auditioned for the solo parts,' she said. 'You were brave and should be proud of yourselves.' Heads turned to Jamila and Eva. This was not good. Jamila wanted to fit *in*, not stand *out*.

'Congratulations to Eva and Jamila,' said Ms Carrington.

Jamila was glad she had Eva with her but she still wished the teacher would stop. Ms Carrington started clapping, and so everyone else did too.

Finn wedged a hand under his opposite armpit and waved his elbow up and down, making no sound at all. Marco patted fingertips together. Only Georgia looked straight at Jamila and clapped like she meant it. Since they had spoken at the solo auditions, Georgia had sat next to Jamila twice during library time and they had talked about the books they were reading.

'Songbird,' whispered Eva. Jamila was grateful, but her stomach churned. It took all her strength not to look in the direction of Alice and Winnie. She wished she didn't care what they thought of her.

Ms Carrington handed out song lyrics and Jamila read the words:

### 'A Voice I Know'

*I am here I wait for you, I see the cars go by*
*But you are not in one of them, and so I wonder why*
*I wait here sometimes all alone, I'm waiting here*
*for you*

*The sky is getting dark, and so my spirit is dark too*

*But hold on now, what is that sound? I hear the*
*doorbell ring*
*There is a voice I know, and now my heart*
*begins to sing*
*I run downstairs towards the voice and see*
*that you have come*
*My waiting days are over, and now I feel the sun.*

Jamila pictured Baba at her door. When would her waiting end?

On Eva's song sheet beside her, Jamila pointed to the word *spirit*. 'What is that?' she whispered.

'Spirit,' said Eva.

'Huh?'

Eva turned to the finger-marked wall beside the piano looking for an answer. 'I think it's… it's…the part of you that no one can see.'

'What is this song about?' asked Ms Carrington.

Jamila knew the ache of missing and waiting. She knew what it was like to move from room to room in a house full of emptiness where Baba should be. She missed the sound of his footsteps, his voice, his laugh.

'Empty spaces,' said Jamila, forgetting to put up her hand.

Everyone looked at her.

Murmured conversation filtered through from a distant room. The hum of cars came in from the road.

'This person who is waiting,' she said, touching the paper. 'They feel like part of *them* is missing.'

'They are waiting for the waiting to end,' said Eva.

She said that like she knew how it felt, thought Jamila. But who did Eva miss?

'Come to the piano,' said Ms Carrington, standing and smoothing her skirt. 'All of you.' She played and sang 'A Voice I Know'. When she sang the song a second time, people began to join in, one hesitant voice at a time. Alice was first, with her chin high, but Jamila heard shakiness in her voice.

After Alice, Miranda joined in, and then Winnie and then Jamila herself. Jamila thought of Baba and Mina as she sang. By the end of the choir session, she knew the words by heart.

Afterwards, Georgia gave Jamila a shy smile on her way out of the hall. Jamila smiled back, pleased to think that maybe she was making another friend. Georgia was holding a notebook and a pencil case. Jamila elbowed Eva and whispered, 'Georgia does homework for more than one hour every night,' she said. 'Do your parents make you do homework?'

Eva looked away before answering. 'I live with my dad,' she said. 'And my aunt. Dad's away a lot. When he's not away, he finishes work late, and he usually comes home after I've gone to bed. I try to stay awake to see him, but that makes him angry.'

Jamila remembered Baba getting cross when she and Mina kept talking past midnight. He had loomed big in the doorway talking sternly as they lay in the dark.

'Aunt Marisa isn't worried about homework,' said Eva. 'So it's up to me whether I do it or not.'

'Me too,' said Jamila. 'Mama doesn't make me, not like she used to. She's too sad.' Jamila hadn't said this to anyone else. It felt good to tell someone. 'She's too worried for Baba.'

Jamila remembered Mama in Baghdad, chasing Jamila up the stairs to do her homework, laughing and clapping her hands in front of her to shoo Jamila to her room. How Mama had changed.

Jamila turned to Eva. 'Where's your mum?' she asked.

Eva ran her fingers through her ponytail and looked around the room before she answered. 'She died,' she said.

Jamila took in a quick suck of air.

'Four years ago,' said Eva. 'When I was seven.' She squeezed the knuckles of her fingers, one at a time. 'She got sick…It's still hard to say it.' Under her breath, she added: 'I don't tell people. They don't know what to say. Then I have to help them.'

Jamila was shocked. And sad for Eva. Just because you live in a safe country doesn't mean your mother can't die, she thought.

That night Jamila thought about Eva and how hard it must be for her without her mum. Jamila had been there when Mina found out that her Uncle Mostafa had been killed. Mostafa might as well have been Jamila's uncle too. He taught her how to ride a bike. He had taken Mina and Jamila to Zawraa Park and to see the Abu Hanifa Mosque in Baghdad. He used to arm wrestle with Baba, and Jamila remembered how he would tip his head back to laugh even when he lost.

There hadn't been any right words to say to

Mina. Uncle Mostafa was gone. Sometimes it felt like death was everywhere in Iraq. So often there was news of someone wounded or missing or killed. People didn't laugh much as they walked the streets—bombs might fall on them, bullets might pierce the air.

There must have been a funeral for Eva's mother with everyone crying and hugging and saying nice things. Jamila was sad for Eva. And she was sad for herself too. She didn't know where Baba was. She had hope, but maybe she would never see him. He had been in prison before. His life had been threatened. Was he safe now?

Jamila tried to get to sleep. She tried counting backwards from one hundred. She turned from side to side until her sheets were tangled. Only when she hummed a song to herself, over and over, did sleep finally come.

# Chapter 9

Jamila sat at a paint-splashed table in the art room. She loved this time of the week. She was good at making things, and she didn't need to struggle as much with her English in art classes. Miss Romney played music—today, two girls sang over a plinking guitar. Jamila tuned in to listen to the words. She hoped there would be no call home from Mama.

Marco and Finn wrestled. Alice and Winnie whispered secrets. Lan stared out the window, probably thinking about her friend. Bethany and Miranda played hand-clapping games. Beza walked around the room, running her fingers over tubes of glitter, rolls of ribbon and paintbrushes up-ended in jars.

'This afternoon,' said Miss Romney. 'We're going to—'

The room was noisy. Jamila cupped her hand to her mouth. 'Shush!'

'Goodie goodie,' said Finn, in a voice loud enough for Jamila to hear, but not Miss Romney.

Jamila regretted saying anything.

'We're going to draw one another's portraits,' said Miss Romney.

Finn groaned.

'Oh. Yay,' said Marco flatly.

Miss Romney gave Jamila a stack of paper to hand out.

'Teacher's pet,' said Beza, not bothering to whisper.

Jamila winced. She handed out the sheets

of paper, and when she reached Beza, their eyes locked.

'My name is Jamila. Call me by my name. I'm not a *pet*.'

Eva was sitting opposite Beza. Her eyebrows rose up.

'Draw an oval shape to fill most of the page,' instructed Miss Romney. 'Like this.' She drew on the whiteboard.

Jamila returned to her seat slowly, even though her heart raced. She knew Beza's eyes were on her.

'Now,' said Miss Romney, 'draw a straight line across the middle. Then, another line halfway between the first one and the bottom of the oval. Between these lines is where you will draw your partner's nose.'

Jamila usually liked drawing people, but straight lines were for drawing tables or houses or robots, not people.

'And then, halve that again and draw your

partner's mouth,' said Miss Romney.

Jamila hovered her pencil over the paper. Miranda was sitting across from her and Jamila was eager to draw her long eyelashes and wispy hair.

'Now, watch,' said Miss Romney. She drew eyes and a nose, and a face emerged. 'The ears are in line with the eyes. And your partner's neck begins at the second line up from the chin.' She added ears and drew two inward-curving lines for the neck.

'Can we colour them in?' asked Beza. She pointed at Eva, and everyone turned to look.

'That scar on her face,' said Beza. 'It's red...or is it pink?'

Winnie gasped.

Jamila fixed her gaze on Beza and pressed her hands into her armpits. 'What is the colour of mean?' she asked.

Eva's eyes opened wide as if she was watching

Jamila juggling six oranges in the air.

'Girls!' said Miss Romney.

'Can Miranda and I draw Eva?' asked Jamila. Miss Romney's attention had shifted to the back of the room where Marco had Finn in a headlock.

'Okay,' she said to Jamila, with angry eyes on Marco. 'That's fine. Fine.'

Everyone started drawing.

Jamila darted quick up-and-down glances over Eva's statue-still face as she drew and forced herself not to look in Beza's direction.

'You're allowed to breathe,' said Jamila. She drew Eva's eyes and brows, her neat nose and fine hair. Then she lightly shaded the area of birthmark across Eva's cheekbone. She stepped back and tilted her head to one side. The lines had helped. The portrait was good.

'It looks like, well, it's great!' said Eva. 'I mean, it looks better than the real me, that's for sure.' Eva pulled her flower-press from her bag, unscrewed the corners and took out three finely pressed orange petals. She swirled glue into one corner of Jamila's paper and stuck them on. She drew the outline of a small cat beside the petals. 'I'm crazy for cats,' she said.

'Nice,' said Jamila.

'I've had this'—Eva touched her cheek—'since I was born. The doctors thought it might fade...' She lifted and dropped her shoulders. 'But it didn't. And it won't.'

'Well,' said Jamila. 'I don't even notice it at all anymore. I just see you.'

But Jamila was angry with Beza. Why had she been so unkind to Eva, pointing at Eva's birthmark in front of everyone? Jamila couldn't stop thinking about it.

At lunchtime the following day Jamila saw Beza sitting in the library with a book open in front of her and she decided to talk to her about it. Jamila tapped her on the shoulder. Beza looked up. To Jamila's surprise, her cheeks were wet from crying and her eyes brimmed with more tears.

Jamila didn't know what to say. Beza looked different, as though she had taken off one mask and put on another. A very, very sad mask.

Beza quickly pulled her sleeves over her hands and wiped her eyes.

Jamila stayed standing beside her.

'My brother,' said Beza. 'I miss my brother.'

'Where is he?' Jamila asked.

'At home,' she said. 'In Ethiopia. He isn't coming.'

Jamila had not thought that Beza might also have family in her home country. And she had never seen this other side of Beza. She was usually fearless and scary.

'Why isn't he coming?' said Jamila.

'He is protesting against the government with other students. He doesn't want to leave.'

Jamila had not thought about Beza's life

outside school. She had only ever seen her come and go from school by herself.

'Missing someone is hard,' said Jamila.

'It's the worst,' said Beza.

Jamila could never forget Beza telling her she should not sing, and her telling Miss Melanie that she and Eva had excluded her when they hadn't. But now, Jamila saw that Beza had worries like her own. She pulled some crumpled tissues from her pocket and held them out to her. 'Find something you love,' she said.

Beza took the tissues.

'To make things better here,' Jamila added. She swallowed. 'For me, it's singing. That's the thing I love.'

Beza dabbed her eyes and cheeks with the tissues. Jamila walked away. She had not said everything she wanted to say to Beza. She had not said that having a friend was the other thing that helped her. And that if Beza could just be nice she might find a friend too.

Jamila decided to go to the secret corner of the playground to find Eva. Now she had two best friends—Eva and Mina.

She remembered Mina helping her to make a purse. Jamila's fingers had fumbled with the thread and she dropped the fox-print fabric. Then she stitched the material to the skirt she was wearing by accident and they had both laughed.

'*La astatee fahmaha, khteer saaba!*' Jamila had said. It's too hard!

Mina told Jamila she should stick to singing and threw a ball of wool at her. Jamila grabbed a pillow off the couch and threw it back, and they chased each other around the room throwing pillows at each other in fits of laughter.

As she crossed the playground, Jamila broke into a run when she saw Eva through the hanging tree branches waiting for her.

# Chapter 10

When Maria, the school receptionist, appeared in the doorway in the middle of choir, Jamila tried to read her face. She was worried Mama had called again. When the song finished, Maria whispered something to Ms Carrington. *No*, thought Jamila. *In shaa Allah, no.*

Ms Carrington did not like anyone missing choir. She beckoned Jamila over. 'It seems that you will not be participating in this session after all,' she said.

Jamila had missed two whole sessions already.

*Damn it! Bloody. Bum.* Swearing felt just as good in Jamila's second language. Ms Carrington looked at her watch. 'Your mother is coming to pick you up.'

A whispered word reached Jamila's ears: 'Again.' It was a girl's voice, but whose?

'I'm sorry,' offered Jamila meekly.

'Off you go,' said Ms Carrington, turning away.

Jamila's classroom was empty when she went to get her bag, and the room felt very different without people in it. She stood behind Miss Dana's desk. There was her cinnamon tea scent, and a late pass with her name on it. Jamila wondered what her teacher thought of her—that she couldn't keep track of time in the mornings? That she was lazy?

Jamila imagined other kids' parents waking their children up in the mornings with bright voices. She saw them bustling in the kitchen as they made breakfast and packed lunches, plaiting their daughters' hair, checking their library bags, sports shoes, excursion forms. Fathers too. Jamila had watched Finn shrug off his dad's parting hug the other day. She had seen Marco and his dad slapping palms together in the air before Marco sauntered away.

Jamila headed for the foyer. Maria looked at her with pity. Jamila felt annoyed, she did not need pity.

'Your mother called,' Maria said.

Jamila held up a hand. 'I know,' she said. 'I *know*.' She marched to the front entrance noisily, stomping past the doors labelled Assistant Principal and Principal. She thought of Mama and clenched her teeth. What was so hard about walking outside and getting on a stupid bus and going to the stupid shops anyway? What about Jamila's life? What about making friends and what about choir?

This time, Mama had called Jamila home to go with her to a Family Support Office appointment. That was worse than shopping. They had already had appointments for health checks, travel cards and for finding a place to live. (They had each been handed a toothbrush, towel and blanket. Jamila could think of better things for starting a new life, like maybe a pet—a guinea pig or a rabbit. But Mama was full of thankyous: *Shukraan. Shukraan. Shukraan.*)

After a train, a tram and a long walk, they reached the Family Support Office—a big grey building. Mama was breathless as they joined the end of the queue. The line crept slowly forward. Jamila wondered if she was the only kid in her class whose family could not buy food or even live in their house without the Family Support Office.

A woman with wire-grey hair called them over. 'Are you looking for work?' she asked

Jamila's mama, running her words together like they were a rug she walked over a hundred times a day. Jamila read her name tag: Vas. She translated Vas's words and Mama's replies, knowing Mama's answers were the *wrong* answers. Her mother was not looking for work. She was not attending English language classes (she had only been to one class!), and, no, she was not enrolled to study. Vas clicked her tongue and typed away.

Jamila thought about choir practice. It would be long over now. The others would have new harmonies, maybe a whole new song. Why did Baba let them come all this way without him? Was he ever coming? Maybe he had just *said* he would come. The thought dawned on Jamila with a sick feeling. She wanted to get out of that building.

'Thank you,' said Vas. 'That's all.' But Mama leant towards her. 'We need—' she pleaded. 'We no have money.'

'I'm sorry,' said Vas. 'You'll have to wait for

the next payment, in a fortnight.'

Mama looked confused.

'Two weeks,' said Jamila quietly.

'Two weeks?' said Mama. 'Please—'

Jamila hated seeing her mother this way. She remembered visiting Baba in prison in Baghdad when one of his eyes was purple and half-closed. Jamila had stayed quiet while Mama begged the guard to let him go. The man held his gun across his chest and stared straight ahead as if Mama was not even there.

Mama looked around at the line of people behind them. Her lips were pale and her cheeks were hollow. Jamila thought about how different she was now. She could remember Mama dressed up to celebrate Eide in Baghdad—she had worn a long, silk skirt, and she had black kohl lining her eyes. She was beautiful and she was happy, with her arm linked through Baba's.

Jamila noticed a family watching them.

'*Hayaa*, Mama,' she said. 'It's time to go.'

Mama's hand was limp in her own as they left the building.

# Chapter 11

Jamila was a morning girl. It was her best time for drawing, for writing songs, for imagining.

She sang to herself as she made her lunch and tried not to think about Mama pleading with Vas at the Family Support Office the day before. She gave Amir his breakfast and propped him in front of the TV.

Where was Mama? She should be up by now. Georgia would be at school already, reading on the steps. Miss Dana would be at her desk, and Winnie would be at the gate, waiting for Alice.

Jamila hated being late. She went in to Mama's room. Mama lay curled on her side under the blankets.

Jamila's hands made fists at her sides. 'Mama!' she shouted. She yanked open the blinds, kicking the wall as if by accident.

Mama rolled onto her back. 'What time is it?' she asked.

Mama used to say she did not need the hands of a clock, she could feel time. This made Baba laugh and wrap his arms around her waist. 'My wife...she can *feel* the time!' he would say.

'It's 8:49!' said Jamila. 'I should be at school.'

Jamila didn't really want to go to school. It wasn't a choir day. She didn't like always being the last to finish her writing, and she was sick of trying to fit in. She looked out Mama's bedroom window at the passionfruit vine climbing up and over the red bricks of the house across the road. She would much rather stay home and write a song.

'Maybe I should just stay home,' she said. 'School is hard. I only have one friend. And I can't understand what the teacher is saying half the time. People think I'm stupid. I *feel* stupid.' She put a hand on her stomach. 'It hurts here, and I want to write a song, and I have decided—I am not going to school.'

Mama sat up. 'Okay,' she said. There was no fight in her voice. 'Okay, *habibty.*'

Jamila went to her room. She changed out of her school dress and unpinned her headscarf. Coffee fumes wafted in from the kitchen. That meant Mama was out of bed. Good.

After breakfast, Mama put Amir in his pram, and they took the bus to the shops. Mama's hand gripped the bar by the door of the bus. Her eyes darted this way and that. In the supermarket, Jamila pushed the pram while Mama filled the trolley.

'What is that?' Mama asked, pointing.

'Sham-poo,' Jamila sounded out.

As she turned into the next aisle, Jamila nearly bumped into a trolley.

'*Mutaasifa!*' said Jamila. 'I mean, sorry!' She looked up at the woman pushing the trolley and recognised Alice's mum.

'Hello,' the woman said. 'Haven't I seen you at school?'

'Yes. I'm in Alice's class.' Jamila put her hand on her throat. 'But I'm sick so I didn't go to school today.'

'Oh, that's no good,' said Alice's mum, glancing at Mama.

In Baghdad, Jamila had missed school when there were air raids, when it was not safe to be in the streets or take the bus. Once, she had missed school to sit with her cousin in hospital after a scrap of bomb shrapnel cut deep into her thigh.

Jamila pictured her empty desk in the classroom, her unopened pencil case, and the blank pages in her writing book. In Baghdad, people had looked up to Jamila's family. Baba was the brave journalist. Mama researched his stories and helped neighbours and friends. Jamila was seen as clever and courageous. Now here she was helping Mama shop for food in a supermarket on a school day, thousands of kilometres from home.

That evening, Mama baked eggplant. Jamila added parsley and yoghurt, then mushed some for Amir. She wrapped a blanket around her shoulders and carried him out to the courtyard. She pointed to the night sky.

'Moon,' she said.

'Moo,' said Amir.

Jamila pointed to her own mouth. 'Moon,' she repeated.

'Moon,' said Amir following the shape of her mouth.

'Yes!' Jamila squeezed him tight. 'Mama!' she

called out. 'Amir said *moon*!'

'Moon,' Amir said again, and Jamila squealed. She tickled his ribs and he giggled.

'Mama! *Ta'ali!* Come!'

Mama came, and Amir said it again.

'What is this word?' asked Mama. Jamila pointed up. 'Moon,' she said.

'Moon,' repeated Mama.

'Moon,' said Amir, and Mama laughed.

'Moon,' they all said together. Amir's first word.


Jamila did not go to school for the next two days either. She felt herself drifting away from her school life—from Miss Dana, choir and Eva. English words floated like feathers from her memory.

When Mama watched TV in the evenings, hungry for news from Iraq, Jamila watched too. The news was not good. Another bomb, rubble, burnt-out cars, shocked and frightened faces. Unwanted memories came to Jamila.

Once in Baghdad, a mosque had exploded into smoke and flames. The air went dark with dust and falling debris, and Jamila's eyes had stung. She had called for Mama and Baba, but she couldn't find them. She had pushed through the crowd and run as fast as she could all the way home. She banged on the door, but no one answered. She sat and waited by the front door, hands shaking, until Mama and Baba finally arrived. Remembering this now, Jamila decided she would not watch the news anymore. She did not want to remember.

Jamila was feeling couped up at home. She took Amir to the park, to play on the grass and swing on the swings. She felt better.

When she got home, she was surprised to see Mama outside waiting for her. 'What is it?' she asked.

Mama handed her a letter and Jamila read fast.

The letter was from Aziza, Mina's mama. It said Baba was safe. He was in hiding but he could not say where. He had applied for a visa to come to Australia, and he was waiting for the Australian government to say he could come.

'Baba!' said Jamila.

'*Amal*,' said Mama. Hope.

'*Ya raab arjook*,' said Jamila. Please God.

'Yes, *ya raab arjook*,' said Mama.

# Chapter 12

When Jamila returned to school, Eva flung her arms out for a hug and said: 'You're back!' Jamila was relieved Eva had not replaced her with a new friend. She had not been forgotten.

'Baba's coming!' she said.

'He is?' said Eva. 'When?'

'It won't be long, now. He's getting a visa. Everyone likes Baba. He's smart—he's writing a book. And he speaks four languages: Arabic, Kurdish, Turkish *and* English.'

'Where were you, Jamila?' asked Eva. 'Have

you been sick?'

Jamila made her voice go quiet. 'Mama needed me at home. And the longer I was away, the harder it was to come back. But now, even though I don't like school, it feels good to be here.'

'Well, I've been by myself a *lot*,' said Eva.

'When Baba comes,' said Jamila, 'Mama won't need me at home so much and I won't have to miss school.'

'Then, I really hope,' said Eva. 'I really, really hope the government likes your dad a *lot*!'


Jamila checked the letterbox every day looking for a letter with more news of Baba. She collected the flyers that were delivered and learnt new words. Her English would be as good as Baba's when he came. It would be any day now. Jamila was sure of it. On the weekend, Jamila made lamb *kibbeh*. She bought a sheet from an op shop, cut it into squares and made a 'Welcome Home' banner.

A week went by, then two, but no more letters came. There were no emails or phone calls either. Jamila sat at the kitchen table. She tried to read the tea leaves in Mama's empty cup. She'd heard you could see the future there. But the leaves were murky and puddled together, and she dumped them into the sink.

'You are strong,' Baba had said. But Jamila didn't feel strong. She was fed up with waiting and not knowing. She had a sudden urge to hurl the sugar bowl against the wall, to make it crash and shatter.

It was three weeks before another letter came from Aziza. The news was good. Baba's visa was approved. He would be on a plane soon. Maybe on the fourteenth or fifteenth of August. Jamila stood still. She circled the dates on her calendar and tried to keep her hope small.

School days dragged. Jamila's toe tapped

rapidly against the floor when a visiting police officer spoke to the class about staying safe. The man in a uniform with a gun in his belt made Jamila want to duck and hide. She could not understand why the rest of the class were behaving like everything was normal. When Finn asked if he could touch the gun, Jamila's eyeballs nearly flew out of her head.

On the twelfth of August, Jamila ran two laps of the local park. She was trying to move time forward instead of waiting. It helped, but not for long.

On the morning of the fourteenth, the sun was barely awake when Jamila rubbed her eyes and sat up in bed. Mama had said Baba might not come that day—they didn't know anything for sure. But Jamila had spent the night half-awake, picturing his face when he saw her, bursting to share all her news. She got dressed and flicked on cartoons for Amir. She shoved a banana and some nappies into the back of the pram. She could hear Mama moving around in her room. '*Yalla*, Mama!' she called. Hurry up! She prepared breakfast of *khubz* with labneh and date molasses, but she could hardly eat and she left most of it on the plate.

Jamila, Mama and Amir caught a train and a bus to the airport. At the International Arrivals gate, Jamila pressed herself against the fence and watched people coming through the doors, wheeling suitcases, carrying babies, pushing trolleys. The people looked into the crowd for faces they knew and the waiting people did the same looking back. A woman jumped over the rail and ran to a man, who dropped his bags and folded her into his arms.

Jamila thought she saw Baba, someone his height and shape, with his forward-leaning walk. She caught her breath, rose onto her toes and leant over the rail to call out.

But it wasn't Baba.

After an hour of standing and watching, Jamila sat down. Soon Mama sat down too, with Amir in her lap.

Late in the afternoon, they went home. Mama cursed Amir's pram when it hit bumps in the footpath. Jamila stepped hard on every crack she could and took a step sideways to crush a plastic bottle with her shoe. *Thwack*.

The next morning, they returned to the airport. They watched and waited. Amir was shuffled in and out of his pram, and Mama walked him up and down in the waiting area. At midday, Jamila kept watch while Mama went to buy some food.

They might have seen a thousand people coming through those doors that day, but not one of them was Baba.

'He isn't coming,' said Jamila.

'He will come,' said Mama.

'I give up,' said Jamila.

'*In shaa Allah*, he will come, Jamila.'

# Chapter 13

The next time Jamila checked the letterbox, there was a letter from her school, addressed to Mrs Safir Hussain. Mama.

Was Jamila in trouble? She tore it open and read it. It was an invitation to a parent information session. Jamila pictured her mother at school with other parents. Would Mama find the right room? She would be shy. And her English wasn't good, she might not understand.

At the bottom of the note were two boxes: Tick Yes ☐ if you are coming and No ☐ if you are not.

Jamila stared at the boxes for a long time. Then she ticked the No box, and scrawled her mother's name on the line beside *Parent Signature*. She folded the paper back into its envelope and pushed it to the bottom of her bag.

At school the next morning, Jamila and Eva sat on the sandpit wall.

'Can I tell you something?' said Jamila. 'You can't tell anyone.'

'Of course,' said Eva. 'What?'

'I've done something…something a bit bad.'

'What?' said Eva.

'Paw-promise you won't tell?' said Jamila, holding up her palm and curling her fingers and thumb inwards like a cat's paw. Eva would never break a paw-promise.

'Paw-promise,' said Eva, touching her own hand-paw against Jamila's.

Jamila unfolded the letter and showed Eva.

Eva sat up straight. 'You faked your mum's signature!'

'Oh, no!' Jamila slapped her thigh. 'You can tell so easily?'

'What else could it be? Am I right?'

Jamila nodded.

'Why didn't you give it to your mum to sign? It's just parent information. They get told stuff about school. Then they probably drink tea and eat biscuits.' Eva shrugged. 'My Aunt Marisa's going.'

Mama wasn't like other mums or like Aunt Marisa. 'Mama wouldn't understand much,' Jamila said. 'Her English is not good. And she has Amir, you know?' The thought of Mama in a crowd of talking parents made Jamila uncomfortable.

Maybe Eva read her thoughts. 'She probably wouldn't want to go anyway,' she said.

'She wouldn't!' said Jamila. 'She definitely wouldn't.'

The signature was a lie. Jamila remembered Aziza's fierce expression when she and Mina had lied about taking money from her purse. They had bought matching braided wrist bands and pulled their sleeves down over their wrists to cover them, but Aziza had found out. 'Lying is *haram*!' Aziza had said, with a jabbing pointed finger. Lying is not allowed.

'I'll tell *you* something I haven't told anyone,' said Eva. 'But it's a giant secret, okay?'

'Okay,' said Jamila.

'At my last school, I wrote my mum's signature on my reading journal every day for ages before anyone knew I didn't have a mum. Before I wanted anyone to know.'

'So, after a while you told people?'

'They found out,' said Eva.

Jamila stretched out a leg to kick over a plastic truck full of wet sand. 'You must miss her.'

'I try to remember everything about her,' said

Eva. 'But mostly I remember her from photos. I feel bad about that, like I should never forget.'

Jamila leant her head on Eva's shoulder and watched clouds moving across the sky.

Later Jamila posted the parent information letter at the school office. She thought about the fake signature as she slipped the envelope into the slot beside the door. Then she drained her water bottle of its last drops. A fake signature was only a *little* bit bad, wasn't it?

# Chapter 14

Jamila was uneasy. What if signing someone else's name was actually *very* bad. Maybe the school would tell the government and Jamila's family would be sent back to Iraq. Or maybe they wouldn't let Baba come.

'Are you okay?' asked Miss Dana, after the recess bell rang the next day.

'Yes!' Jamila blurted. 'What? I mean, why? I'm good.'

'Is everything okay at home?'

'Yes,' Jamila replied, very quickly.

'Jamila, look at me,' said Miss Dana.

Jamila looked.

'You know you can talk to me if there's anything worrying you.'

Jamila forced her mouth into a smile. 'I'm fine,' she said.

Jamila helped Mama shop for extra food on the weekend, so she wouldn't be called home from school. She shoved all the dirty washing she could find into the washing machine and turned it on. When it finished, she hung the clothes on the clothesline out in the courtyard. When there was no more space, she hung Amir's jumpsuits and singlets on the backs of chairs. She did all her homework. By Sunday evening, she lay on the couch with her eyelids drooping while Mama sang Amir his bedtime lullaby, *'Nami, nami'*. Sleep, sleep.

At the end of the next choir session, Ms Carrington invited Jamila into her office and closed the door behind her. 'You are one of the strongest singers, Jamila,' she said.

'I love to sing,' said Jamila. She felt jittery. Why was she in this room?

'Lately, you have not quite been yourself,' said Ms Carrington. 'You forgot your lines this morning. It's not like you.'

Jamila had been trying to act normal since she wrote her mother's signature. But now Ms Carrington was asking questions.

'I'm sorry,' said Jamila. 'I…'

Ms Carrington's phone rang. 'Excuse me,' she said, turning away to talk.

Jamila thought about the signature. What would happen next? She sang to herself to escape the worry.

When her call ended, Ms Carrington asked, 'What was that you were singing?'

'Just now?' asked Jamila.

'Yes, just now—what were you singing?'

'A song I wrote. It's called "My Faraway".'

'Would you sing it for me?'

Jamila used to sing her songs for Mina and for Baba and Mama. She was pleased that Ms Carrington wanted to hear her song. But the room was so quiet, and the signature hung in her mind. At first, she sang haltingly, in a small voice. But soon singing relaxed her the way it always did, and she sang in her full voice and even let her hands go out at her sides when she held the long, last note.

Ms Carrington's eyes glistened and Jamila wondered if a tear might slip out. 'Did you write that song yourself?' she asked.

'Yes,' Jamila said. She didn't feel so worried about being in Ms Carrington's office any more. *Singing does that*, she thought. *It takes worries away, like a magic trick.*

Jamila also understood there was something

special about 'My Faraway' because she had felt a kind of electricity when she was writing it. As if the words and the melody came *through* her from somewhere else.

'Would you like to perform "My Faraway" at the concert?'

'Sing my own song? Yes!'

'How lucky we are to have you,' said Ms Carrington.

Jamila smiled a great beam of a smile and clutched her hands together behind her back.

Jamila's class had lying-down meditation first thing the next morning. Chairs were stacked and desks pushed against the walls so that everyone could spread out. Jamila lay on the floor next to Eva. She spoke in whispers and told Eva everything about singing to Ms Carrington after choir. Eva turned on her side and propped on one elbow.

'Just you and Ms Carrington were there?'

'Yes,' said Jamila.

'Were you nervous?'

'I was at first. But once I started singing, I didn't feel scared any more. I was just...singing. And now she wants me to sing my very own song for my solo!'

'Wow,' said Eva. She rolled onto her back. 'You're a real songwriter now.'

Photos of the class in the bush and at the beach were pinned around the door frame. Jamila liked this school. She read the 'About Me' posters that were stuck to the wall.

My name is Winnie. I am good at fractions and bad at spelling. Animals are more important than people. People who eat them should be eaten by lions. I wouldn't even kill an ant.

Hi. I'm Finn. I hate asparagus and I'm a soccer pro. This morning my sister found weevils in her muesli. She screamed and I laughed.

'Feel your belly rise as you breathe into it,' said Miss Dana. Jamila closed her eyes and thought about singing her song in the concert. She imagined Mama's face in the audience. Then she remembered Baba and she was worried again. He should be there. How could she sing at all without him in the audience?

'When you start thinking about other things,' said Miss Dana, 'just go back to feeling your breath going in and out.'

Jamila's shoulders relaxed. She felt her arms and legs sinking into the carpet. And she fell into a deep and dreamless sleep.

She woke to Eva saying her name and pressing her shoulder. 'Wake up, Jamila. We're finished.'

# Chapter 15

The phone was ringing when Jamila arrived home after school. She fumbled with her key in the lock. Could it be the man who rang about Baba? Jamila dropped her bag and nearly tripped over it in her rush to get to the phone.

'Hello?' she said.

'Hello. Can I speak to Mrs Safir Hussain, please?' It was a woman's voice.

'Who is it?' asked Jamila.

'My name's Leyla. I'm from Refugee Support Victoria.'

Jamila didn't like the word *refugee*. 'I'll get Mama,' she said.

Mama was in the kitchen.

'Refugee what?' Mama asked, grimacing. Maybe she didn't like the word either.

'Tell her no thank you.'

Jamila returned to the phone. 'Mama says, no thank you.'

'Oh, tell her I come from Iraq,' said Leyla. 'Tell her the Family Support Office gave me her number. We help families who are new to Australia.'

'What kind of help?' asked Jamila.

'Learning English, other things. It's your mother I need to speak to.'

Jamila went back to Mama. 'She's from Iraq, she says she can help.'

Mama took the phone. When she broke into Arabic, her words flowed. When Mama asked if Leyla could help bring Baba to Australia, Leyla must have said no because Mama's mouth pressed shut like it did when she was not happy. Mama listened for a few more minutes and then she said she had to go.

'What did she say?' asked Jamila, after Mama hung up.

'She can't bring Baba to us.'

Jamila sat down and frowned. The woman was offering help. 'Mama,' she said. 'I don't want you to keep calling me home. It makes school harder. And Leyla can help you learn English. She speaks Arabic.'

Mama scratched at a stain on the table with her fingernail.

'You can drink tea with her,' said Jamila. 'And I will make biscuits.'

Mama cupped Jamila's cheek with her hand. 'You are a good daughter. I will try.'

'Yes!'

Jamila went to the library that afternoon and found the phone number for Refugee Support

Victoria on the internet. She wrote it down and handed it to Mama when she got home.

Mama kissed her on her forehead and picked up the phone.

Jamila listened as a visit was arranged. Leyla would come the following Monday afternoon. After Mama hung up the phone, Jamila gave three quick claps.

Jamila spent the weekend cooking and making the house nice. She loved to cook for people. She had been making cakes since she was eight years old without even looking at a recipe—date and pecan, lemon and sugar. Sometimes they came out of the oven flat and hard, but other times they were just right, and when Baba took giant bites the crumbs caught in his beard.

For Leyla's visit, Jamila made biryani, yoghurt dip and ginger-and-date biscuits. Then she swept the path out the front. A man and his dog walked past.

'G'day,' said the man.

'G'day,' said Jamila. And she practised again, when he was out of earshot. 'G'day.'


On Monday after school, Jamila heard knocks on the front door.

'She's here!' she called. '*Yalla*, Mama.' And she opened the door.

Leyla looked relaxed and friendly. She wore an orange hijab, and her hands were tucked into the pockets of her pants. She introduced herself.

'Come in!' said Jamila, excited to share the food she had prepared. She brought out tea and biscuits and put them on the table.

Mama told Leyla her days at home with Amir were long. She said shopping was not easy because she couldn't always read the labels or find the ingredients she needed—okra, leeks, barley. She worried for her husband.

Leyla sat forward with listening eyes.

When Mama went to the kitchen, Leyla turned to Jamila. 'How is school?' she asked.

'Okay,' said Jamila. 'I'm in the choir. My teacher is Miss Dana. And I have one friend, Eva. But...' Jamila hesitated. 'Mama needs me here. A lot. So...'

'Are you missing school?' Leyla asked.

Jamila gave a tiny nod. 'Mama doesn't like to go to the shops without me. Or anywhere, really. It's hard for her even to get up in the morning sometimes.'

When Mama returned, Leyla took a card from her purse and put it on the table. 'Safir,' she said. 'There is an Iraqi woman—a volunteer. Her name is Alina. She can come and teach English. And go with you to appointments.'

'*Shukraan*,' said Mama. Thank you.

But when Leyla left and the door clicked shut behind her, Mama went to her room leaving the card where it lay.

# Chapter 16

When Jamila arrived at school, Miss Dana asked her to go to Mrs Ward's office.

'Mrs Ward?' Jamila shuddered. She had only just shoved her schoolbag onto a shelf. 'The principal?'

'Yes,' said Miss Dana. 'The principal.'

'Go!' said Eva. 'Maybe it's a *good* thing—you know, about your song in the concert!' Eva always thought of good things first.

Jamila went with Miss Dana down the hall and past the staffroom.

The principal's door was ajar. 'Come in, Jamila. Please sit down,' said Mrs Ward.

Jamila had never seen Mrs Ward look so serious. She had joined in drama games with her class and pretended to be a pirate once. When they had Italian, she would call out *'Ciao!'* or *'Buongiorno!'*

But today, the corners of Mrs Ward's mouth were pulled down. She held the parent information letter. Jamila could see the signature that she had written at the bottom.

Mrs Ward slid the letter across the desk to her.

'Now, Jamila, who wrote this?'

Jamila had to cough to find her voice. 'I did,' she said.

Mrs Ward raised one eyebrow.

Jamila had seen Finn raising one eyebrow and then the other to make Marco laugh. She felt like giggling now. She also felt light-headed. For once, she was glad Baba was not here.

'It's my mother's name but I write it,' she said.

'*Wrote* it,' corrected Mrs Ward.

'Wrote it.'

'So, you *pretended* your mother signed the letter.'

Jamila lowered her gaze to the desk.

'I see,' said Mrs Ward.

Jamila hated anyone to think she had done the wrong thing. She was always trying to do the right thing.

'I pretended to be my mother. I signed the letter,' said Jamila. 'I didn't...'

'Signing a document with another person's name is wrong, Jamila,' said Mrs Ward. 'Do you understand?'

Jamila understood she was in trouble. She had made everything worse. A knot formed in her throat.

'Why did you sign the letter?' asked Mrs Ward.

'Mama is...I didn't want...' Jamila couldn't find the words to explain.

The beeping of a reversing truck filled the air. It was too loud, and went for too long.

'I have rung your mother about this, and she is on her way here.' There was a new softness in Mrs Ward's voice and that made Jamila want to cry.

Jamila sat outside the principal's office waiting for Mama to arrive. The carpet under her shoes was worn down to its last threads. Who else had sat outside this door waiting for whatever trouble they had to face? The minutes stretched on forever. Would Mama come to the school quickly, or would Jamila be left sitting on the world's hardest chair for hours? She tried to picture Mama getting off the bus at the right stop and then at the front desk, asking where the principal's office was. She watched the shadow of tree branches moving across the wall until, finally, Mama did arrive.

First, Miss Dana appeared with Amir on her hip. Then came Mama.

'I'm sorry, Mama,' said Jamila.

'*Madha faelti*?' said Mama. What have you done? But she squeezed Jamila tight.

Mrs Ward showed Mama the letter and the signature.

Mama looked anxious. There was a new layer of fear and worry in her eyes.

Jamila knew what Mrs Ward did not know. Mama had bigger worries. And now, because of Jamila, she had another problem she would not know what to do with.

# Chapter 17

When Jamila got home from school, she wrote in her notebook:

*I try to be someone people like. I try to show the teachers I am clever, but English is hard and everyone thinks I'm not smart. Baba would not be proud. Mama's English is not getting better and what can she do without English? Without words, you can't live in a place with other people. You live in a room with a closed door and never come out.*

*I miss Mina and I'm scared that maybe now Eva won't want to be my friend. Australia is a safe place, but I am always fighting.*

She lay on her bed and pulled the blankets up to her chin. When she fell asleep it was late afternoon, and she dreamt she was on stage. Alice, Georgia, Winnie and Finn were in the audience. Jamila stepped up to the microphone and opened her mouth to sing but no sound came out. Finn pointed and laughed. And then Baba appeared. He watched and waited. Still, she couldn't make a sound.

When Jamila woke up, her room was dark. She flicked on her bedside lamp and sat in front of the mirror with her chin in her hands. Her skin was pale and her hair was a mess. She rubbed her eyes and combed her hair with her fingers. She could smell fried onions and spices and her stomach groaned with hunger. She went to the kitchen.

Amir was in his highchair at the kitchen table. His hair was damp, and Jamila smelled shampoo when she kissed him. Mama brought out *sheikh mahshi* stew and rice with almonds, Baba's favourite dish. The spicy smell reminded Jamila of him. Mama seemed different, she had made a special dinner. Jamila was glad.

For a while, they ate in silence. Jamila thought of past dinners, with music filling the room, Baba singing along, and Mama and Baba talking about their day.

'Jamila, *alresala kanet lee*,' said Mama. The letter was for me.

Jamila stopped eating.

'*Ana umeky.*' I am your mother.

Jamila raised her hands. 'I didn't want to give you any more problems.'

A neighbour's dog would not stop barking.

Jamila's eyes met Mama's. Jamila could see that Mama was cross but also that she didn't want to be.

'You have to learn to speak English,' said Jamila. 'You only went to one English class and you never went back. And we *do* need help.'

Mama closed her eyes for a beat. 'I know,' she said.

Jamila sat up in surprise. Mama had said it in English. *I know.*

A breeze came through the window and stirred the air. The room felt different, like something good was coming.

Later that night, Jamila looked through her desk drawer for a photo of Baba. Instead, she came across the card Leyla had left.

Leyla Mohamud
Refugee Support Victoria
27 Scott Street, Preston, 3072

She knew Scott Street. It was next to the market. One tram trip, and a short walk. Jamila wedged the card into the side of her dressing-table mirror and climbed into bed. She lay wide awake and thinking until a plan was clear in her mind.

Early on Saturday morning, Jamila asked Mama if they could go to Preston Market.

'I want to make *tashreeb dajaj*,' said Jamila. 'Aziza used to make it, and I really miss Mina and Aziza.'

Mama said they needed vegetables so, yes, they would go.

They took the tram, and when they got off Jamila led the way, taking a detour down Scott Street. Her heart revved as they approached number twenty-seven.

Jamila stopped in front of the Refugee Support sign and turned to her mother. 'Let's go in,' she said.

Mama read the sign. 'Jamila, *ayna nahnu?*' she

said. Where are we?

'This is where Leyla works. This is where we can get help,' said Jamila.

Mama looked like she might say angry words or storm away. But Jamila felt strong. 'Please,' she said firmly. Something had to change in their lives. Maybe Leyla was the key to that change.

Then Mama did the strangest thing. She sat down. Then she leant against the wall and dropped her head into her hands. And she cried.

Jamila sat beside Mama. The ground was cold. It was hard seeing Mama cry.


Soon, Mama wiped her eyes with her sleeve, stood up and smoothed her skirt. Jamila stood up too.

'Okay,' said Mama. 'Go ahead. Press the buzzer, *habibty.*'

Jamila pressed the buzzer, and they waited.

Leyla opened the door. She invited them in and introduced Mama to Alina.

Mama talked and listened, leaning in to Alina as she spoke. Jamila chewed her finger tip. Mama was talking, and she sounded a tiny bit like her old self when she was speaking Arabic. Maybe she was making a new friend. Maybe she would get better, more like she used to be.

Alina offered to help Mama to learn English, and to come to appointments to help with translation. Mama said yes, that would be good. Jamila felt like crying though she didn't feel sad. If Alina helped Mama, then Mama might not call Jamila home from school so much. She couldn't wait to tell Eva all about the meeting.

Mama hugged Alina before they left. Jamila felt lighter. She breathed slowly in through her nose and out through her mouth.

Then, she had an idea.

# Chapter 18

Jamila called her school early on Monday morning and asked to speak with Miss Dana.

'Is everything okay?' asked her teacher.

'I took Mama to see Leyla.'

'Leyla?'

'From Refugee Support. She is so nice. Mama talked to Leyla and to Alina. Alina is a volunteer. She helps people when they come to Australia from other countries. And now, I think Alina will come to our house to help Mama learn English while I'm at school, and go with her to appointments.'

'This is good news, Jamila.'

'Miss Dana, I want to ask you something.'

'What is it?'

'I shouldn't have lied. I shouldn't have signed Mama's name.'

'No, you shouldn't have.'

Jamila put her hand on her hip and stood up straight. 'I want to talk to Mrs Ward. It's not good that I am in trouble. I want to explain. I want her to understand.'

'Well, of course. I will speak to Mrs Ward and arrange a meeting.'

What *would* Mrs Ward say? She was the *principal*. She was the boss of the whole school. Jamila was just a kid. She looked out to Mama in the courtyard. Mama held Amir's hands as he tried to take steps. He had been trying for weeks. His whole body wobbled as he took one step, and then another. His tiny fists were white where they gripped Mama's hands. How Jamila loved Amir.

As soon as the bell rang for recess the next day, Jamila and Eva went to Mrs Ward's office. Mama was already there, waiting outside with Amir. The meeting was scheduled for 11:15 and it was now 11:12. Jamila pulled her headscarf closer around her face. The hijab she had chosen was one of Mama's, in serious shades of brown. Her school dress was clean and ironed. She slid her thumb over the face of her watch, thinking of Baba. What if he could see her now?

'I'm nervous,' Jamila said to Eva.

'You *asked* for a meeting with the principal,' said Eva. 'You're number one, Jamila.'

Jamila put a hand to her throat. 'Is this crazy?'

'Yes. *Good* crazy. I wish I was like you.'

'You want to be crazy?'

Eva laughed. 'I want to be brave.'

The principal's door opened, and warm air flowed out around them.

'Come in,' said Mrs Ward. She reached out to

shake Mama's hand. 'Welcome, Safir,' she said.

Mrs Ward was taller and wider than Jamila remembered. She had a gold owl brooch with ruby eyes that seemed to blink at Jamila.

Jamila had written down the exact words she wanted to say. But now, she was unsure. Her stomach dipped like it had when there was turbulence on their flight to Australia. Only this time, the turbulence was made up of her school principal, Mama and, at the centre of the turbulence, *causing* the turbulence, Jamila.

'Hello, Mrs Ward,' said Eva, nudging Jamila. Jamila was glad Eva had been allowed to come to the meeting.

'Good morning,' replied Mrs Ward.

'Hello,' said Jamila, in barely more than a whisper.

Baba had always encouraged Jamila to speak for herself. Now, as if Baba was here and urging her on, Jamila led Mama, Amir and Eva into the principal's office, and they sat down in the chairs by Mrs Ward's desk. There were papers and folders on the desk and a filing cabinet stood against the wall. Jamila imagined a thick file with her name in bold capitals in one of its drawers.

'How are you, Jamila?' said Mrs. Ward. 'What would you like to talk to me about?'

'I know I did the wrong thing when I signed the letter,' said Jamila. Her heart jumped wildly in her chest.

Mrs Ward dipped her head, as if to say keep going.

'I did the wrong thing,' said Jamila. 'But I did it for the right reasons.' She was glad she had practised this line and the lines to come. 'I go home from school many days to help Mama. I go with her to the shops, to appointments, to the doctor.'

Mama dropped her gaze to her lap.

Jamila didn't want Mama to feel bad, but she needed to tell the truth. 'Mama doesn't have many

English words,' she said.

Jamila could feel Eva beside her, and she knew Eva believed in her. Knowing this helped her keep going.

'I thought,' said Jamila, 'if Mama came to the parent information session, she wouldn't understand. Maybe she would feel ashamed. I don't want Mama to feel ashamed.' Jamila's mouth was dry. 'I wish I hadn't signed the letter,' she said. 'But I can't be in trouble. I don't want the government to know what I did. We *can't* go back to Iraq.'

'She can't!' added Eva, hooking her arm through Jamila's.

Mrs Ward held up her hand. 'No one is telling the government anything, Jamila. No one is sending you back to Iraq. You did the right thing in coming to talk to me.'

Then Mama spoke. 'Jamila is a good girl,' she said to Mrs Ward. 'She tries. Always, she tries. She does homework. And she helps me at home. My

English...' Mama didn't finish the sentence.

'We can organise an interpreter for you,' said Mrs Ward. 'And we can have the parent information translated into Arabic.'

Jamila was surprised. She didn't know the school could help.

'You can do this?' said Mama.

'You are part of our school community,' said Mrs Ward. 'We want to make our community stronger.'

Mrs Ward was being nice to Mama. Did she still think Jamila was bad?

'*Shukraan*,' said Mama.

'Mama said thank you,' said Jamila.

'My door is always open,' said Mrs Ward.

Eva stayed close beside Jamila as they left. Jamila knew that later they could talk over every word she had exchanged with Mrs Ward. She wanted to run out of there with Eva and swing on the swings or climb a tree or go to their hidden corner.

# Chapter 19

Jamila and Eva met up at the bridge in Galleon Lake Park on Saturday morning. The park was halfway between their houses. They leant over the timber railing, and Jamila took a pebble from her pocket and dropped it into the water. It made a small plonk and disappeared.

'I can't wait for the concert!' said Eva. 'What are you going to wear? Ms Carrington said bright colours.'

'Baba bought me a blue dress for my eleventh birthday,' said Jamila. 'It has a black sparrow on one shoulder. I'm going to wear that. What about you?'

'Aunt Marisa found red overalls in an op shop—they're exactly my size,' said Eva. 'And red is my favourite colour.'

Jamila began to sing 'My Faraway'. *I'm looking out, I'm looking out, the ocean goes for miles...*'

Eva joined her here and there, dipping in and out of the song, her voice in perfect harmony with Jamila's. They tried different things. Sometimes Eva's voice would go up high on the words that were important. Jamila thought it made the words stand out. On the chorus, Eva sang softly underneath Jamila's voice, and it seemed to give the words more feeling.

'That sounds good,' said Jamila.

Eva nodded. 'It *feels* good too,' she said.

They practised some more, going quiet only when people came close as they crossed the bridge.

Then they'd pick up from where they left off. They stayed on the bridge and sang 'My Faraway' over and over until the sky changed to a deep blue and Jamila thought Mama might be worried about her. 'I better go,' she said. 'But let's sing together again.'

'Yes,' said Eva. 'I can't believe the concert's next week!' She turned and skipped away.

'I'm so excited!' Jamila called after her.

# Chapter 20

The sun was pushing through the clouds on the day before the concert. Jamila was both excited and nervous. What if she forgot the words or tripped over on the stage? When Jamila had sung at school in Baghdad, Baba, Mama and Mina were in the audience and she had seen herself as they did—a brave girl with a beautiful voice. Baba said Jamila had a voice like bells. Mama said Jamila's singing made her remember things. Now Jamila would sing in her new school. She would sing in front of her whole school and neither Baba nor

Mina would be there. But Eva would be with her and Mama would be there. Jamila would sing for Mama—to remind her to wake up and be happy. She wanted Mama to feel something good.

Jamila was too excited to eat when she got home that afternoon. Mama sat her down at the kitchen table. She said she had something important to talk about.

'Aziza sent an email to my friend Zainab and now—'

'Yes?' said Jamila, shifting to the edge of the seat. She was thinking about singing with Eva on the bridge—she wondered if Ms Carrington would let Eva sing harmonies with her at the concert. They could practise some more before school in the morning.

'Uncle Elias is coming to Australia, maybe tomorrow,' said Mama. 'He knows where Baba is. He can tell us when he is coming.'

Uncle Elias used to crawl around on his hands and knees with Jamila on his back when she was little. He had shown Jamila how to draw owls and eagles using chunks of charcoal that had left her fingers black.

'In the morning,' said Mama. 'We will go to the airport.'

Jamila stood up so fast the table wobbled. 'But the concert!' she said. 'It's tomorrow morning! At ten o'clock! Did you forget?'

Mama stood up too. Now they were standing face-to-face.

'Uncle Elias is family, Jamila,' said Mama. 'Family is number one—did *you* forget? There will be other concerts.'

'Other concerts? What other concerts? This is my *school*, Mama. I am there every day. This is my *life*. I can see Uncle after the concert!'

Jamila wondered if her uncle was really coming anyway. The thought of watching more strangers coming through the arrivals gate for nothing was unbearable.

'I do not have time for this, Jamila,' said Mama. 'Not another word.'

Jamila's shoulders tensed and her brow creased. Her chest rose and fell quickly with her breaths. She was furious.

That night, Mama polished her shoes. She washed her best skirt and ironed it until it looked new on its hanger. She would not meet Jamila's eyes.

Jamila could not believe this was happening. What could she do now? No one else Jamila knew from Iraq had come to Melbourne. Uncle Elias spoke the same language and ate the same food. Mama had a photo of him holding Jamila as a baby, beaming like she was a prize he had won. She was excited he was coming. It was a good thing. But of all days, why tomorrow?

While Jamila got dressed in the morning, thoughts

crisscrossed her mind. She didn't know what to do. She had never defied her mother before, not in a big, important way, but she wanted to now. She put on her blue dress with the bird print on the shoulder. She wore navy tights, sparkling slip-on shoes and a silk headscarf. Ms Carrington was expecting her. Eva was expecting her. The stage was empty but soon there would be a microphone set up. The thought gave Jamila a sinking feeling.

Uncle Elias was on the plane, flying to Melbourne. Mama had made the couch up into a bed for him. When Amir tried to climb onto it, Mama pulled him away.

'Eat quickly, Jamila,' she said. '*Yalla.*'

Jamila wasn't hungry. How could she eat at a time like this?

They walked to the train station. This time, Mama took the lead. Jamila pictured the choir singing without her, and she felt like the air was being sucked out of her.

They arrived at the platform with a two-minute wait for the next train to the city. From there, they would take a bus to the airport. Jamila felt the sharp edges of her travel card in her hand. The seconds ticked slowly by. Jamila's mind raced. A train clattered around the bend and slowed to a stop in front of them. Mama pushed the pram towards the nearest doors.

'I'm not coming, Mama,' said Jamila.

Mama stopped still. 'What?'

'I can't miss the concert. The bus stop is that way'—Jamila pointed—'and it isn't far. I will go straight to school.'

'But, Uncle Elias—' said Mama.

'I will see him after the concert,' said Jamila.

Mama looked to her hands gripping the pram and shook her head. She turned to Jamila. 'You know the way?' she asked.

The door beepers sounded.

'Yes, I really do.' Jamila's heart walloped in her

chest. 'I'm not getting on the train. And you don't have to worry.'

The doors slid open.

Mama fumbled in her bag and took out her phone. 'Here,' she said. She looked flustered and cross. She told Jamila she would find a way to call her from the airport to make sure she had arrived safely. 'Go to the bus stop. Don't talk to anyone.'

'I won't,' said Jamila, excitement bubbling inside her.

Mama tilted the pram and pushed it onto the train. The doors slid shut behind her and Jamila saw only herself in the window's reflection.

# Chapter 21

The train pulled away and Jamila was alone on the platform. The concert was set to start at 10:00, and it was 9:37. She wished she had worn runners.

She ran out of the station towards the bus stop.

What would Mina think of Jamila leaving Mama at the station? The answer came easily—she would say *Sing, Mutraba!* Jamila ran past the lolly shop and the crumbling house on the corner, past the apartments with the giant iron gates. She bolted over the bridge in the park and took shortcuts down backstreets.

She outran a yapping dog and almost tripped on a jutting piece of footpath. When she saw her bus pulling into the road, Jamila waved and shouted.

The driver stopped for her. Jamila's breath was tearing in her chest as she ran for the doors. She clambered on and fell into the nearest empty seat.

When she arrived at the school hall just after 10:00, the concert had not yet started.

Eva's arms landed around her neck. 'Jamila!' she exclaimed.

'You're here!' said Georgia.

'We thought you weren't coming,' said Miranda.

'I couldn't miss the concert,' said Jamila. 'I couldn't.' In her mind she could still see the train doors closing behind Mama.

Just then, Mama's phone rang in Jamila's pocket. Jamila answered. It was Mama asking if she was at school.

'Yes,' said Jamila. 'I'm here.'

'Okay,' said Mama. 'Okay.'

Jamila could not tell whether Mama sounded angry or relieved. She wanted to ask if they were with Uncle Elias. She wanted to say she was sorry, but Mama hung up quickly.

'I am *so* glad you're here!' said Eva. She wore her red overalls and she had a flower tucked behind one ear. It was good to see her.

'We heard you faked your mum's signature,' said Marco.

'I did,' said Jamila. No more lies.

'We thought you were in trouble for missing so much school,' said Winnie.

'I've been missing school to help Mama, my mum,' said Jamila. She was tired of trying to hide the truth. There. It was out. And the world had not stopped turning. Her classmates had not turned and run away from her.

Mama was probably fretting about Jamila now.

Or was she just plain angry?

Ms Carrington came over. She was wearing a knee-length black dress. Studs sparkled in her ears. 'I'm pleased to see you, Jamila.'

'Oh, well…yes. I'm here now.'

'Are you ready to perform your solo?' asked Ms Carrington.

Jamila blinked hard to focus on the concert. 'Yes,' she said. 'But—can Eva sing with me? She can sing harmonies, and she knows all the words.'

Ms Carrington pinched her chin between finger and thumb. 'You have devised harmonies?'

'Mostly in the chorus,' said Jamila.

'And at the end,' said Eva.

'Really?' said Ms Carrington. 'Well, I do hope you've practised.'

'We have,' said Jamila.

'Thank you!' said Eva. Eva had lost a front tooth the day before. There was a gap when she smiled. Jamila felt a rush of affection for her.

A crowd was gathering at the hall entrance. Chairs had been set out in rows all the way up to the stage.

'Oh, my god,' said Winnie. 'There are so many people.' She ducked behind Alice as if to hide.

Finn pointed in the direction of the crowd and started counting out loud.

'Stop it!' said Alice. 'You're making me nervous.'

Finn kept counting.

Miranda finger-combed her fringe down over her eyes and folded her arms.

Georgia was reading song lyrics to herself, with her mouth moving silently.

'It's time,' said Ms Carrington.

Jamila took her position in between Eva and Georgia in the semicircle on the stage. There was an uncomfortable knot in her stomach. She wished Mama was here, but not angry. She wished she was here to see her in the concert.

Jamila's palms tingled. She wanted to tell Eva everything about her morning but there wasn't time. Parents and brothers and sisters were streaming in, followed by all the students who were not in the choir. When the audience settled, Ms Carrington introduced the choir and sat down at the piano.

Alice rose onto her toes to reach the microphone, and Jamila thought of Mama stepping onto the train, picturing the back of her shoe just before the doors slid shut.

'This song is called "A Voice I Know",' said Alice.

Ms Carrington played a chord. Alice sang the first lines alone, timidly. Then Jamila, Eva and Winnie joined her. Everyone came in for the chorus and Jamila forgot, at last, the train doors closing behind her mama. Her voice and the voices of the others carried her along. How she loved to sing!

Miranda introduced the second song, about a winding road to home. A tall man made his way along the back row towards an empty seat. Eva waved to him and the man waved back. Eva's dad, thought Jamila, and she scanned the faces of the audience, from the girl passing an apple from hand to hand at the front to Maria standing with Mrs Ward at the back. No Mama. Of course, no Mama. Why even look?

Jamila's song was next. She stood with Eva at the microphone ready to begin. And then she saw her coming into the hall—Mama. She had made it! She was there! And she didn't look cross.

Following Mama, and holding her hand, was a man. A man with a beard and a leather satchel over his shoulder. And his hand holding Mama's.

Was it Baba? It couldn't be. Jamila looked closer. He was thinner and his beard was flecked with silver. His eyes met Jamila's and shone.

'Baba!'

Jamila jumped down off the stage and ran to him. 'You're here!'

Baba took Jamila into his arms.

Jamila breathed in his familiar smell of spices and coffee, and he held her tight, tight, tight.

'*Al Hamdu li'Allah*,' said Baba. Thank you, God. With his hands on either side of Jamila's face, he gently touched his forehead to hers. Jamila closed her eyes and the crowded room dissolved away.

'I have something for you,' said Baba. He reached into his satchel and took out the fox-print purse Jamila had only half-sewn at Mina's house in Baghdad. Mina had finished it and stitched a single word onto the front.

مطربة

'*Mutraba*,' Jamila read. 'This is from Mina.'

Baba nodded.

There was the sound of many people talking at

once from the crowd. Then another man crouched in front of Jamila, with a wide smile that crinkled the corners of his eyes.

'Uncle Elias!'

Elias embraced Jamila and kissed the top of her head. *'Hadha yawm saeid,'* he said. This is a happy day.

Baba glanced at the stage. *'Yalla*, Jamila. Sing for us.' Jamila held the purse tight and ran back to the stage to Eva's side.

She looked out at the audience and saw Baba take his seat beside Mama. Was Jamila dreaming? She struggled to stop herself from laughing and crying at the same time. Then, she took a deep breath and closed her eyes to think of what to say.

She swallowed back her tears. 'This song is for Baba...my dad. I...' The words stuck in her throat.

Eva leaned in to the microphone. 'Jamila wrote this song. It is called—'

Jamila chimed in and the two girls said the

words together: '"My Faraway".'

Jamila's voice soared and Eva's harmonies dipped in and out and together their voices filled the hall. They sang past the ceiling and through the windows out to the playground. They held everyone in the room with their song.

When the song came to an end, the mums and dads in the audience wiped their eyes. Everyone, especially Mama, Baba and Uncle Elias, whistled and clapped. Miss Dana whooped, students pummelled the floor with their feet as they cheered, and the choir took a bow.

When the audience began to leave the hall, Jamila took Eva by the hand. 'Come!' she said, and she took Eva to meet her family.

'This is Baba. My dad!' she said. 'Baba, this is my friend, Eva.'

'I am very pleased to meet you,' said Baba. Jamila could still hardly believe this was happening.

'And this is my mama!' Jamila searched

Mama's face to see if she was angry.

Mama kissed Eva lightly on her cheek. She looked at Jamila and her face showed just a hint of disapproval. 'I cannot be angry,' she said. 'But Jamila, what you did was not okay. Never again.'

Jamila let herself exhale.

Uncle Elias held out a hand to shake Eva's. 'I am Jamila's favourite uncle,' he said.

'Hello,' said Eva.

It seemed to Jamila that her two worlds were coming together before her eyes.

'We must celebrate,' said Mama. Her smile was big and bright.

Together, they all went back to Jamila's house and opened blinds and windows. Jamila put on dancing music, and Eva helped her to put food on the table.

Jamila held her arms out and spun in a circle. '*Al Hamdu li'Allah*,' she said.

# Three Weeks Later

On the first Saturday morning in spring, Jamila and Eva walked through Preston Market with Baba, Mama and Amir. Jamila wore Mina's fox-print purse around her neck. Baba carried a backpack filled with capsicums, eggplants and berries.

'I have news, Jamila,' said Baba.

Jamila stopped walking and looked up at him. 'What is it?'

'Mina's family has applied for visas.'

'To come here?'

'Yes, to come here,' said Baba. '*In shaa Allah.* We hope they will come.'

Jamila felt like running along the aisles of the fruit and vegetable stalls and throwing lemons into the air. 'Mina! My Mina!' she cried, lifting Amir high into the air. She turned to Eva. 'You will love Mina!'

At a nearby stall, they sat to share *knafeh*, sweet cheese pastry with crushed pistachios soaked in sugar syrup. Jamila licked her fingers. 'We must buy chicken and limes,' she said, holding up a sticky finger. 'Eva and I want to cook today. I want to show her how to make *tashreeb dajaj.*'

'*Na'am, habibty*,' said Baba. Yes, my darling.

'Leyla and Alina are coming for dinner tonight too,' said Mama.

'Your English, Safir...' Baba splayed his hands out in front of him. 'I think you have been taught by the best.'

Mama laughed. 'It's true,' she said.

'We will make a feast!' said Jamila.

'*Na'am*,' said Eva. Yes.

'*Yes*,' said Jamila. 'A feast!'

# Glossary

A list of Arabic words in *Songbird**

| | |
|---|---|
| *abnatay aldhakiya* | my clever girl |
| *ah'sant* | well done (for a male) |
| *ah'santi* | well done (for a female) |
| *al hamdu li'Allah* | thank you, God |
| *alresala kanet lee* | the letter was for me |
| *amal* | hope |
| *ana umeky* | I'm your mother |
| *binafsi* | by myself |
| *bismillahir rahmanir raheem* | in the name of Allah |
| *dajaj* | chicken |
| *habibi* | my love, my darling for a male |
| *habibty* | my love, my darling for a female |

| | |
|---|---|
| *hadha yawm saeid* | this is a happy day |
| *haram* | forbidden |
| *in shaa Allah* | God willing / if it is God's will |
| *khajul* | shy (for a male) |
| *khajulla* | shy (for a female) |
| *khubz* | a type of flatbread |
| *kibbeh* | minced lamb croquette |
| *knafeh* | sweet cheese pastry |
| *la astatee fahmaha, khteer saaba* | it's too hard |
| *la naerif 'ayu shay* | we don't know anything |
| *lays al'an* | not now |
| *madha faelti* | what have you done? |
| *mudahash* | amazing |
| *mutaasifa* | sorry |
| *mutraba* | a girl who sings / songbird |
| *na'am* | yes |
| *samoon* | a type of bread |
| *shukraan* | thank you |
| *ta'ali* | come |
| *tashreeb* | to soak |

| | |
|---|---|
| *wallah* | by God / I swear to God |
| *yalla* | hurry up / let's go / come on |
| *ya raab arjook* | please, God |
| *ya rab* | oh, God |

*These translations are based on how the words are used in the story. Just as in English, some words would have different meanings in different sentences.

# Acknowledgments

Thank you to Anna McFarlane and my agent Clare Forster, for helping me to find the right home for *Songbird*. And to the team at Text Publishing, especially Jane Pearson, for being that home and bringing Jamila's story to life.

Antoni Jach, I so appreciate your guidance and the opportunities you create for writers. Hilary Rogers and Helen Chamberlin, thank you for your input and enthusiasm when this story was just a spark.

I'm grateful to Amal Alsoubut, Nuha Hariri, Zaid Edward, Saleem Aljebori and Hajir Al-Gburi for your encouragement, feedback and language skills.

To my writing community, you are invaluable. Special thanks to Madeleine Jenkins, Chris Miles, Lachlan Jacobs, Marion Roberts and Rachel Power.

Mum, thank you for always being a willing reader and for feedback on early drafts.

Josie, your enthusiastic support has been wonderfully helpful. Dad, Bec, Stefan and Al, you're the greatest. Thank you for always having my back and egging me on.

Special thanks to my brilliant teaching friends and colleagues at the Collingwood English Language School. And to my beloved friends Naomi Taig and Julia Messenger, who prop me up again and again.

And to Benny and Mia, thank you, as ever, for your love and support, and for being my pack.